Praise for

Ashe Barker

This second entry in the The Dark Side Trilogy is just as good if not better than the first. Instead of getting some back-story then taking off, Darker begins right where Darkening left right off at (Thank God!). Boy I was not disappointed. ~ *Reviewed by Jeep Diva*

Totally Bound Publishing books by Ashe Barker:

The Dark Side
Darkening

Sure Mastery
Unsure
Sure Thing

The Dark Side

DARKER

ASHE BARKER

Darker
ISBN # 978-1-78184-662-9
©Copyright Ashe Barker 2013
Cover Art by Posh Gosh ©Copyright August 2013
Interior text design by Claire Siemaszkiewicz
Totally Bound Publishing

Published in 2013 by Totally Bound Publishing, Newland House, The Point, Weaver Road, Lincoln, LN6 3QN, United Kingdom.

Totally Bound Publishing is an imprint of Total-E-Ntwined Limited.

DARKER

Dedication

This book is dedicated to Lisa, for showing me how it
might be possible, and to Hannah, for convincing me
it was.

Chapter One

Mist. Dim, cloudy, swirling. Pain, intense pain, burning, searing pain. A voice, harsh, angry, cursing words. Lifting, moving. "No, stop, please... Hurts."

"Sorry, angel. Christ, I'm sorry. Lie still, let me help you." Soft, comfortable, gentle hands, soothing, cool.

"Aah!" More sharp pain intruding, spearing, trust-breaking. I sob, struggle. I need to escape.

"Easy, love, you're going to be okay, I've got you..."

Darkness again, sweet, silent darkness. I float, drifting, escaping...

* * * *

I wake. The room is in semi-darkness, the heavy curtains closed to shut out most of the sunlight. I am face down, lying on top of the duvet on Nathan's huge bed. I lie still, listening. Silence. But I sense I'm not alone.

The first forgetful moment of wakening slips past and I start to remember, to recall what happened. The sofa, tied down, helpless, exposed. And the cane, the beating. Jesus, the sheer mind-numbing paralysing agony of it. Then it stopped. I must have passed out. Nathan must have released me, carried me to the bed.

He was there then. I start to recapture bits of memory, pulling the threads together. I remember Nathan's voice, shocked, then angry as he realised I was losing consciousness, then nothing as the black fog covered me. I'm pretty sure I heard 'Holy fucking shit'. Then nothing.

Then, much later perhaps, his hands, his arms lifting me, hurting again. My fear, my desperation to escape, to be safe. His soft words soothing, his gentle hands spreading healing, cooling cream over my tender skin. Him rousing me when I wanted to sleep, when I wanted to drift away. I don't want to return, to be hurt anymore. Asking me my name. Asking me where I am. At last, satisfied, he let me be. I remember drifting away again, peaceful now, resting, sleeping.

And now I'm awake, and he's here somewhere. Not talking. Watching me, perhaps. I stir, try to move, but the pain overwhelms me again. I groan, lie still. Where is he? Where's Nathan? I need to talk to him. I need to tell him what I think of him and his bloody games. The bastard. The heartless, vicious, fucking bastard.

"Eva?" His soft, tender voice sounds close to my ear. I can feel his breath, whispering across my hair. I turn my head, face him.

The words of accusation tumble out, unchecked. "You promised not to hurt me. You promised to take care of me. You... You..." His deep, chocolate eyes are, if anything, more pain-filled than mine, but I'm not letting up. I'm driven by unexpected disappointment. *In me? In him?* And by a self-righteous sense of betrayal. I spit my words at him. "You bastard. You total and absolute bastard. Sadist!"

He's crouching beside the bed, at my eye level. He doesn't back away in spite of my anger. Neither does he retaliate, seek to defend himself. He just gazes at me.

"What date is it today, Eva?"

"How the fucking hell should I know? Go buy a newspaper. And drop dead while you're at it."

His wry smile only serves to enrage me further.

"Fuck off. I hate you. I hate you." The last words are sobbed, my anger spent suddenly, giving way to grief. He reaches for me, pulls me into his arms. And I go. Unresisting, I cling to his black T-shirt, sobbing noisily. "I was scared. I was so scared... I thought I was going to die." My voice is small, no more than a whimper. He just holds me, stroking my hair, my shoulders and my back.

"You're not dead, love. Nowhere near. I'm sorry, though, it was my fault, I should have seen... You should have told me. Why didn't you tell me?"

"I don't know. I don't know. I couldn't... I just couldn't." Incoherent, I just cling on, my tear-stained face buried in the fabric of his T-shirt. He doesn't press the matter. Not now. Not yet.

Embarrassed, confused, my head in turmoil, I retreat into my normal mode of defence. Myself. "I want to be on my own for a while. Please."

"I'm not sure..."

"Please. I need to think. I need to sleep. Please, just leave me on my own for a while."

Not convinced, he's frowning at me. Then he relents, slightly, "All right. But I'll be downstairs. In my office. And you, you don't go anywhere. Understood?"

"What? Where would I go?" Bewildered, I stare up at him. I'm in no condition to go gadding about bloody Leeds, that's for sure. The man's an idiot as well as a sadistic bastard. *Just my luck.*

His smile, gentle, tender, suggests he knows what I think of him at this precise moment and has some sympathy with my views. "Okay, I'll go, leave you in peace. For now. But I'll be back in a couple of hours. No more." He gestures with his head at the table beside the bed. "Your phone's there. Text me when you wake up." He stands, looking down at me for long moments before adding, "Eva, we need to talk about what just happened. Really talk. You scared me. I thought… I thought… Shit. We need to talk."

I don't answer, just pull myself over to lie on my side, my back to him. I hear him cross the room, hear the door close gently behind him and at last I am alone with my thoughts. I close my eyes again, and I sleep.

* * * *

And now I'm awake, and find myself perversely wishing he was still here. I should never have sent him away. I need to apologise—I let him down. I let me down. I need to know we're okay.

I struggle to push myself up onto all fours, not yet trusting myself to be able to sit. The pain has subsided to a sharp sting, but I'm sore, very sore. I need to get to the bathroom, shower, get a drink of water. I shuffle sideways to the edge of the bed, ease my legs over, then get my feet connected with the floor. I carefully, slowly, push myself up into a stand, grabbing the bedhead for support. I wait for my head to clear, for my knees to lock, ready to carry me.

A note. On the pillow next to where my head was. A note in a small white envelope. My name on the front. *Eva*.

He's gone. Not far, only downstairs. I sent him away. But he left me a note…

I pick it up, turn the envelope over in my hands, then drop it to the duvet as I suddenly need to rush for the bathroom. I get there in time — just — and heave up my guts. This is getting to be a habit in moments of stress around Nathan. The nausea isn't going away any time soon. I spend the next half an hour clinging to the side of the toilet, making a disgusting spectacle of myself.

Eventually, weak, feeble, fragile, I totter back to the bed. I realise I am still naked. Bruises have started to develop on the backs of my wrists. I guess I must have been straining against the straps as he caned me. So much for leaving no marks. There's a mirror on one of his wardrobe doors so I stagger over there, twisting my body to see the damage to my bottom.

It is strangely unscathed, just three or four light pink stripes to show for my ordeal. I test the marks with my fingers. The skin is tender, stings slightly, but otherwise I seem to be okay. Desperately relieved, my confidence in Nathan marginally starting to recover, I go back to the bed. I sit down carefully, shifting to test my throbbing bum. It's bearable.

I pick up the envelope and without giving myself time to think I slide my thumb under the flap to tear it open. I pull out one sheet of A5 paper, handwritten.

Eva
I'm downstairs if you need me. Text me when you wake up to let me know that you're OK.

If you're awake by then, I'd like to see you in my office at 4.30 p.m. James is expecting you.

You scared me. I was so worried about you.

Eva — You have some explaining to do, starting with what you consider to be meant by the concept of safe word.

Nathan

Shit. He was so kind before, so gentle. Contrite even. I don't need to see his angry face, hear his harsh words to know he is livid now. An anger born of fear maybe, but I will be getting the full force of it. Soon. I know I've screwed up. Badly.

I glance at the clock—it's quarter to four already. I scramble for my phone, text him quickly as instructed, keeping it cheerful.

Hi, Nathan, I'm awake now, a bit sore but fine. No need to come back up. I'll be there at 4.30. Thanks for looking after me. See you soon.

Then I head for the shower.

Twenty hot, steamy minutes under the powerful jets of water help to relax my stiff body and I feel the kinks of tension easing as the warmth permeates. I'm feeling a lot less delicate as I scout around the spare bedroom, rummaging in my Harvey Nicks carrier bags for something decent to wear.

As my equilibrium returns to something more akin to normal, I'm reliving the whole bizarre episode and wondering how the hell it all went so wrong. I may be a bit flaky sometimes, naïve even, but I'm far from stupid. Very far indeed. It was simple enough—all I had to do was say 'stop'. Or 'red'. Or something like that. And I can't deny I had my chances—he did ask me if I was okay.

What was I thinking? By the tone of his note, that's pretty much what Nathan will be wondering as well, and I have no idea at all what I'm going to say to him.

At twenty-five past four, I slip out of the apartment. I cross the landing and press the lift call button. I have dressed myself carefully for the occasion in one of my new outfits, smart beige chinos with a floppy black silk blouse. I am tempted by the fuck-me red heels again but decide not to be too obvious and settle for shoving my bare feet into my black Toms slip-ons. I have my small black leather satchel for my bits and pieces — glasses, phone, tissues, a few quid in cash and my somewhat under-used credit card. The lift arrives quickly, and I am on my way to the eighth floor.

Exiting the lift, I approach James' desk again, and if anything I'm even more nervous than yesterday. At least then I'd thought Nathan would be pleased to see me. Today, well, who knows?

James sees me, smiles and picks up his phone. "Miss Byrne is here, sir." After a moment he replaces the receiver and smiles up at me. "Mr Darke is expecting you. Please, go straight in."

The door to Nathan's office is closed. I walk up to it, and decide against knocking. I walk in, before closing the door quietly behind me. He is at his desk, his eyes riveted to the screen of his laptop, his fingers leaping across the keyboard. His hair, loose when I saw him last in the bedroom of his apartment, is now scraped back into his severe businesslike ponytail. I stand, leaning back on the door, unsure what to do now. The obvious place to sit would be at the conference table, but the sharp recollection of being stretched across its polished surface yesterday and beaten with a ruler makes me hesitate. I'm unwilling to take a seat at *that* table but not sure if my legs will carry me right across the room to the visitor's chair in front of his desk.

Long moments slide by as he makes me wait. He appreciates the importance of timing, I'll give him that. Whether he's about to deliver a withering dressing down like now, or a severe beating across my naked bottom like earlier, he knows the added value of making me wait. Giving me ample time to anticipate. To dread. Eventually he looks up, his dark eyes boring into mine. Still he doesn't speak. I swallow—my mouth dry. If he seemed harsh, cold the night we met, he is positively glacial now. Christ, he's so very, very angry. And I'm so very, very scared.

Defensively I try to convince myself it's all his fault. If he doesn't want me to pass out and spoil his fun, he shouldn't hit me so hard. A glance into that icy gaze and any bravado I might have been gathering is splintered.

"Come here, Miss Byrne. Can you sit?" He gestures at the chair in front of his desk. I nod, then walk hesitantly to him, before easing my body gently into the chair. His expression is wry—he knows how sore I am. "Backside smarting, is it, Miss Byrne? Good." He shoves his laptop aside. I have his undivided attention now, and he goes straight for the jugular. "So, Eva. Safe words. What are your safe words? What are they for? And why the fucking hell didn't you use them?"

I stare at him, open my mouth intending to speak, but belatedly I realise I don't have an answer. At least not one he'll be interested in hearing. Does he really want to hear how I was paralysed by pain, unable to move, unable to speak or scream? How, somewhere buried in the fog of my brain I knew I had a solution? How I knew I could stop the agony, somehow, but forgot what I was supposed to do? To hear how pain and desperation and fear drove all sensible thought from my head? How I could only lie there until he beat me senseless?

No. I need to come up with something better. I think for a few moments, desperately casting around for something, however flimsy. Unfortunately, there really isn't anything better, anything more convincing. There's only the truth. And that's it. So that's what he'll have to make do with. I open my mouth again, take a deep breath in a futile attempt to steady myself, and this time I tell him. The truth. All of it.

He listens quietly. His face is a mask of incredulity. An expression of utter disbelief—I assume, at my stupidity—drives all else from his handsome face. Or maybe he's just completely astounded by my sheer bloody feeble weakness. He doesn't interrupt, waiting until my voice trails away before delivering his reaction. And it is not sympathetic.

"You *forgot*. You wanted to tell me to stop, but you *couldn't*? That's fucking not true. I asked you. I stopped, I waited and I bloody well asked you if you were okay. God knows how many times, I asked you if you wanted to stop. I was totally focused on you and I thought you might be struggling. I asked you if you were okay to continue. You told me yes so I carried on." His voice is cold, his words crisp, clipped, his temper only just reined in.

The door opens behind me and he falls silent, though his angry glare holds me in place, pinned to my seat like a specimen butterfly. I hear James come in, then the clink of coffee cups as he places a tray on the table. The table where Nathan gave me twenty blistering strokes with a ruler then followed it up with a mind-blowing orgasm. My lower body starts to clench. The sensations, and my response to him, no less powerful for being remembered.

"Thanks, James." Nathan's voice is chilled, clipped as he dismisses his PA.

"Right, Mr Darke." And he is gone, leaving me once more alone with the very angry, very, very intimidating Nathan Darke. If Nathan with a whip in his hand seemed formidable, Nathan in an ice-cold seething temper is positively awesome, crushing. Am I cowering? I think I might be. If not, I should be. And I suspect I soon will be. I try to salvage something from the carnage.

"It won't happen next time," I offer earnestly. "I'm a fast learner." *That's true, I'm probably one of the fastest learners on the planet.*

"You don't need to learn. You just need to fucking understand a simple instruction and Do. As. You're. Told." The words are forced out through his gritted teeth. "Was that too much, Eva? What part of 'tell me when you want to stop' was not entirely clear to you?"

His sarcasm is cutting, unkind and, in my view, unwarranted. I feel my temper start to kindle a little, fighting back. "Damn it, you mean, clever bastard." Is that my voice? Is that me being so rude? Yes, apparently so. How odd... Still, I'm in now so I rush on.

"I'm new to all this, or had you forgotten? How was I to know how I might react to the shock of having some sadistic pig thrash me senseless with a bloody cane? I know now, thank you so very much for the educative experience. I'm so obliged to you. And you needn't worry, I've learnt my lesson. I'll get it right next time." I am standing, leaning over his desk, shaking with anger, with defensive outrage at his callousness. I might see fit to blame me for this mess, but somewhat perversely I don't see why he should.

The thing is, if I'm totally honest, I do blame myself. He did stop and check. He did remind me, repeatedly remind me, of the safe words. I could have called a halt. I could have slowed everything down, managed my pain better. I could have, should have got through it, and claimed my reward in the form of another mind-blowing erotic experience. Then we'd both have been out of our minds with delight. But I just let him beat me till I passed out. Nice one, Eva.

He shakes his head, slowly, sadly — his lips turned down, flattened in disappointment. He leans back, no longer aggressive and judgemental, just disillusioned. My flash of anger subsiding, I start to panic. I've seen that look of upcoming rejection before as those around me have realised I'm not for them, not like them, not one of them.

I sit, ready to grovel now, my short burst of self-defence exhausted. "Please, Nathan, can we —"

"If you can't manage to use safe words to protect yourself, to protect me too, damn it, Eva, then you can't play these games. It's too dangerous. Sooner or later I'll hurt you. Really hurt you. I could end up in jail, you in the hospital or the undertaker's. So it stops here."

I am staring, the blood drains from my face, my head is swimming, spinning. "No. No. It can't be. Another chance, surely I deserve that. Everyone gets another chance..."

I realise I must have said it out loud as he answers me, more gently now, "It's not about chances, Eva, it's about keeping you safe. As the Dom that's my responsibility, and I just can't do it if you don't tell me when you need me to stop. Otherwise I'm just shooting blind. Taking risks. Taking big risks with your safety. So no, Eva, no more chances."

"You're dumping me. Over this. It was your fault, and now you're dumping me." I know I sound hysterical, hyperventilating like a child on the verge of a tantrum, but the sheer agony of this heartless rejection is choking me. I need him. I need this. I need what he can teach me. I flinch under the sudden pain. The grief, the sense of loss is overwhelming. Unbearable. I am crying, my face in my hands, sobbing just as I did last night as I relived the bitter pain of losing my father. This is just the same, another bereavement, my heart is being torn from me. I love him, like I loved my father. But he's leaving me anyway. Like my father did. I can't bear it. I just can't. I can't even start to contemplate my future without him in it.

"I wouldn't call it dumping you, Eva. I care about you..." *Platitudes. Spare me, please!*

Desperate, I'm ready to grovel, to plead. "Please, Nathan. Please don't just send me back to Black Combe. Not yet. Let me try again."

He has the grace to look uncomfortable, to shift in his chair as he picks up a slim file from the desk. "Ah, well it's not that simple. About Black Combe... I'm not sure you can go back there either."

The pain is sharp, physical, the pit of my stomach dropping away. My job. My new home. My new friends—all gone, gone because of this. Because he couldn't keep his hands off me, because he was so determined to lay into me with a cane and I made one little mistake. No. It can't be. I don't believe this.

"Why?" I whisper, wide-eyed, bewildered in my grief and confusion.

He pushes the file across the desk to me. "Your certificates. Your birth certificate and your music degree. I had them checked out. They're forgeries. Or one of them is. Which one is it, Eva?"

"What? What are you talking about?" I stare at him, astonished. "They're both genuine. You can check."

"I have checked. That's the problem. The dates don't add up."

Ah, yes. The dates. I had hoped he wouldn't notice, wouldn't look too closely. More fool me. Of course he would. Bloody attention to detail control freak. As my silence lengthens, he continues, explaining, "Your birth certificate — which seems genuine, incidentally, so I'm inclined to think the degree certificate is the fake — says Evangelica Byrne was born in Edinburgh in April 1990. Yes?" He glances at me for confirmation. I nod dumbly, obligingly.

"And this degree certificate says that Evangelica Byrne was awarded the BMus degree by King's College London, in 2005. First class honours no less. Impressive, but not possible Eva. You were only fifteen in 2005." He waits, tapping his long fingers on the sheet spread out in front of him.

I sit, my eyes fixed on my shaking hands, twisting them in my lap. I can explain. I can. He'll think I'm a freak, but that's no worse than the rubbish in his head now, what he thinks he knows about me. He thinks he's caught me cheating, lying. And that's why he wants to fire me from my job. At least I might be able to salvage that.

I look him in the eye. "Both documents are genuine." With a deep breath, I continue, "I entered Kings in 2003, when I was thirteen. I got my first degree two years later, in 2005, when I was fifteen as you say." I sit still, waiting for him to react. He shakes his head. He doesn't believe me. Shit, I'll need to prove it, and that could mean—will mean—all my cats out of their little bags.

"You're a superb violinist, Eva, I don't doubt you do have a degree in music. Why bother to forge one? You could play professionally…"

Yes, I could, I've turned down more offers than I can remember…

"But at fifteen—no university would even accept a student at that age, let alone have one graduating."

I take a deep breath, square my shoulders and look him straight in the eye. "They do, if the student has an IQ of one hundred and eighty-one, seventeen GCSEs and counting and eight A levels. Do you want to check those certificates too?"

I have the intense satisfaction of seeing his jaw drop. For a few moments he seems truly speechless then he regroups a little.

"But why? Assuming it's all true, what was it all for? I mean, three or four A levels makes sense, five even at a stretch. But eight? And how many GCSEs was it?"

"Seventeen. Then. I've picked up a few more since. I've been half expecting to be invited to the AQA exam board's office Christmas party, I'm so well known there…" I break off, conscious that I sound like a total freak, and here I was trying to convince him I'm fairly normal.

"But why, Eva?" Far from reassuring him of my status as a normal person, Nathan's expression is one of absolute bafflement. And I really have no convincing answer to his question. Still, I have to try.

"Because I could. And it's what people like me do, sort of a hobby. I love to learn things, new things, so I'd go from subject to subject, reading, practising, whatever was needed. I only ever need to read something once, and I remember it, absolutely. No need for revision or anything like that so it really doesn't take that long. At school they kept on entering me for exams, and I kept on passing them. The challenge wasn't so much to pass, it was more about getting the A* grades. My school also offered a degree level curriculum so I had a head start. I did the equivalent of the first year of my degrees in maths and music while I was still there, but there comes a point when you just need to move on and get into a university..."

My voice trails away, and I'm still not totally convinced that he believes me. He is staring at me, then back at the documents in front of him. Time for my trump card. "Can I please borrow your iPad?" He slides it across the desk to me. I fire it up and go online, navigating quickly to my own Flickr account. I find the photo my proud mother took at my degree ceremony—me a lanky little teenager, dwarfed among the strapping twenty-somethings, all lining up to shake the chancellor's hand. "That was me in 2005," I say, passing back the iPad. He stares at the screen and mutters something sounding rather like 'Fucking hell'. Then, 'That investigator's fired'.

I reach for the iPad, intending to close the thing down, but he has other ideas. Just as I knew he would, he Googles me. The most obvious way to find out the key facts in anyone's life. And my key facts come up. And just keep on coming. And coming.

I watch his face, his eyes skimming down Google's list of Evangelica Byrne mentions, of my accomplishments. It's a long list. He scrolls down, keeps looking back to my face, one eyebrow quirked. Eventually he's done, the iPad at last blank. Now he's just gazing at me, his expression unreadable.

"Well, you are a lady of many, many talents it would seem, Miss Byrne. Except it's not Miss Byrne, is it? It's Dr Byrne. Am I right?"

I nod.

"Tell me. Tell me from the beginning. How did you get to do all, all this…?" He gestures at the small black screen, pressing the on switch to bring it all back up again.

"As I said, I have a high IQ. So I'm a fast learner."

"Lots of people are fast learners. Even I can be when it suits me." Another inscrutable stare — I'm not sure if I'm being threatened or not. He goes on, once more reading down the Google list. "This is more than just being quick on the uptake. Don't hedge with me, Eva. Tell me about yourself. All of it. Now, please."

"Okay." I take another deep breath, close my eyes to gather my thoughts, and work out just where to begin. He waits. He's patient and not going anywhere. So, at last, I start.

"I am, was, what the educationalists would call 'profoundly gifted'. That means I have an IQ of more than one hundred and eighty."

He interrupts me. "You said one hundred and eighty-one. And I'm guessing that makes you some sort of fucking genius? What about the average person, someone like me? What would their score be?"

"I've no idea about you. Actually you don't seem at all average to me."

"Are you insulting my penis again, Dr Byrne?"

"God, no!" My head snaps up, I meet his eyes and realise he is smiling, joking with me. He seems to have an unerring gift for knowing just when, and how, to lighten the mood — help me to relax, to get my story out. It works, and I continue, feeling slightly more confident now. "The average score is around one hundred, the normal range is about twenty points above or below. Ninety per cent of people fall into that range."

"So at one hundred and eighty plus you're well outside the range of 'normal'?"

"Yes. My score is one hundred and eighty-one." I say it quietly, and want to explain, justify myself. "I don't normally tell anyone that—it seems, well, it seems like boasting. But you did ask me. And the truth is it's not always that great to be so far outside of the 'normal'."

"Oh? How's that then? I can see being a slow learner would be a struggle. So how was it for you, Eva?"

"Starting school was awful. I was so bored. I got into lots of trouble, even got expelled—permanently excluded in the education jargon—for being a troublemaker, disruptive."

"Miss Byrne, disruptive. Now I'd really like to have seen that." His gentle smile is encouraging. Maybe he'll listen, accept me, even after all that's happened. Hoping, daring to let myself think this whole pile of crap might turn out to be okay after all, I continue.

"My mother was brilliant. She knew what was wrong with me, or right with me, depending on how you see it. She knew what I needed. She'd seen me learning to read, all by myself, before I was three. She kept asking my schools to have me tested, but no one would, they just thought I was a nasty, attention-seeking little tearaway and she was a doting mother who could see no wrong in me. Maybe she was, but she was also spot on about my 'special' educational needs. My dad's RAF career meant we moved a lot and schools just thought I was reacting to that, never getting settled anywhere. It was only after he died, when we moved to London and stayed put at last, that my mother paid for me to be assessed by a private school specialising in gifted children. They repeated the tests three times before they accepted my scores. Then they offered me a place, on a scholarship because I was a 'special case'. From then on I was fast-tracked through the education system. I started taking GCSEs at around nine years old, passing them, obviously, and then A levels. By the time I was thirteen I had armfuls of GCSEs and A levels. My school said I was wasting my time there and I needed to move on. To university."

"How did you cope, at university so young? How did you make friends, take care of yourself?" Typical Nathan, straight to the heart of the issue.

"I didn't. That's why I'm the screwed up mess I am now." At his puzzled look I press on, anxious now to get all this out. "I went to universities in London so I could live at home, like any other thirteen-year-old." I noted his eyebrow quirk again at the mention of universities, plural, but we'd come back to that. "I was so much younger than the other students, I had nothing in common with them. I couldn't go to bars. I had no interest or talent for sport. I hadn't even started my periods so how could I relate to the other girls, much less the boys. Actually, I was terrified of the boys. My mother always warned me to stay out of their way, that they were dangerous and would take advantage of me because I was so young. Looking back I understand her concerns, but I got it fixed in my head that boys, men, were to be avoided. So I avoided them. In fact the other students, males and females, were generally kind enough, when they took any notice of me at all. But mostly I was the little nerd at the back. The strange, brainy kid, who went home every day for her tea."

"What about other kids your own age? Kids at your school?"

"At my special school I was okay, I did make some friends there, although the catchment for the school was so wide—most of southern England—that I had no friends living near me, no one to socialise with outside of school. So I never did socialise. And in any case the friends I had were left behind when I went to university. I've had acquaintances since, colleagues, but no friends. Until now. At Black Combe. That's partly why I so want to keep my job. Please."

"The jury's still out as far as your job with me's concerned. I want to hear the rest of this then I'll decide. Please, continue." He stands, walks around me to the table, squeezing my shoulder as he passes me. I take that as an encouraging sign and listen to him pouring coffee, before he brings me a cup. Instead of sitting back behind his desk, though, he grabs a chair from the meeting table then turns it to face me. He sits down just a foot in front of me. Feeling more vulnerable, more exposed than I have during any of our sexual or Dom-sub encounters, I sit still, staring at my hands. I can feel his eyes boring into me as he considers. Then taking my hands in his, he squeezes them until I look up at him. He smiles.

"I can see this is difficult for you. Take your time. I'm listening."

I close my eyes briefly, starting to relax—slightly—and I rush on before he thinks better of it. Best to get my academic CV dumped on the table, so to speak, and let him pick over it. Work out just what sort of a weird bitch he's got mixed up with.

"I studied music at King's because I loved it. It was easy, light relief really. But music was the second string in my bow if you'll pardon the pun. Really, I was a mathematician. I got the first class BMus, but I also got a first in Mathematics the same year." His eyebrows shoot up again—apparently a mathematician is to be viewed with even more respect than a gifted violinist. "The two sets of skills are often found together," I hasten to explain, somehow wanting to reassure him that I'm not that special, not that odd. Not really. "Then I moved to University College London, did an MSc in Mathematics and Modern Languages. I was awarded that in 2008, when I was eighteen."

"So, a musician, a mathematician and a linguist. There really is no end to your remarkable talents, Miss Byrne. Sorry, Dr Byrne."

Sarcasm? But he is smiling. His eyes are smiling. He really doesn't mind. "So, what did you do from 2008 to now?"

"I went back to King's, this time into the Faculty of Modern Languages. I got a research fellowship, and did my PhD in Linguistics. Then in 2010 I was offered a research fellowship at Oxford, St Hilda's College, and that's where I was until a few weeks ago."

"So, Dr Byrne, it sounds as though you've had a glittering academic career. Why did you leave?"

Ah, the six million dollar question. The one I still struggle to answer. But I'll try. For Nathan, I'll try.

"I wanted more in my life than just academic institutions. I've never been anywhere else, done anything else except learn, study, research and occasionally teach. I like to teach, but I don't get to do it that often…"

My voice trails away. The next bit is the hard part. This is where I become vulnerable again, my emotions and needs laid bare. I reflect on the irony — I've already laid my body bare before Nathan, and on balance he's looked after it pretty well. Apart from that one mishap, for which I do accept some measure of responsibility. But emotional fulfilment is a whole new ball game. Men are not good at emotional stuff, at the touchy feely stuff — or so I understand. But hey, who am I to talk?

"I... Growing up I got the education I needed, eventually. Some of it. Most of it. Intellectually I matured, and I am now a respected academic in my field." *Well, several fields really.*

"Physically too. I may not have much in the way of curves and sex appeal, but I am a normal woman, everything works fine. Even my libido, as I now know."

"How fortunate for us both, Dr Byrne." His smile gives away the humour behind the wry statement, encouraging me to go on.

"But emotionally, I'm a bit of a car wreck." Leaving that hanging in the air, I stop, take a sip of my coffee to give me a moment to work out what to say, how to explain my particular pile of mangled wreckage. The liquid hitting my stomach reminds me that, apart from a croissant at breakfast — which he rudely interrupted to spank me — I haven't eaten all day. My stomach growls loudly, taking both of us by surprise.

"Sorry," I mutter, pressing my free hand to my grumbling tummy in the hope that it will just keep quiet long enough to not disgrace me further.

Laughing, he takes my coffee cup and puts it on his desk. "I want to know all about your car wreck, Eva. I suspect that's the heavy stuff and we *will* deal with it.

But first we need to feed you. And have some fun, I think. Some light relief. Do you fancy a night out? Or rather — will you come out with me tonight, Eva?"

Incredulous, I gape at him. "Are you asking me out? For a date?"

"A date? Yes, could be. Will you come out on a date with me tonight, Eva?"

"No one's ever asked me to go on a date before. I'm not sure…"

"I'm beginning to realise how sorely lacking your otherwise brilliant education has been in some important respects, Miss Byrne. Sorry, Dr Byrne. There are some gaps. Some very worrying gaps. Gaps we need to fill. And dating is one of those gaps. I agree that in an ideal world the dating would come before the fucking, but hell, you've got to start somewhere. So, Dr Byrne, will you come out with me tonight? Please."

Laughing, I begin to get into the spirit of it. "Yes, Mr Darke. I'd love to. Where are we going?"

"Hey, we're in Leeds, cultural centre of the known universe. Well, Yorkshire anyway. What do you fancy? Opera? Ballet? Theatre? Cinema? Clubbing? Casino? Dancing?"

"Not clubbing, definitely. And I've got too many aches and pains for dancing just now. And anyway I can't dance."

"You'll learn. But not now. And later if you're very well-behaved I'll massage those aches and pains for you if you like… A bit more gentle fucking perhaps?"

My heart leaps, delighted, relieved. He still wants me. Amazingly, he still wants to make love to me. "I'm not dumped then? You said… I thought you meant…you didn't want me anymore."

"You were never dumped, Eva. Not really. And I want you so much I've a few aches and pains of my own. But you did terrify me and we do need to sort out the safe word business. I can't do with you fainting like a Victorian virgin every time I pick up a cane. My heart won't stand the strain."

"Well I was very nearly a virgin. And I told you, I'm a fast learner. Maybe now you'll believe me."

"True on all counts, Dr Byrne. You are extremely well-qualified. But please allow me to be the authority on gentle fucking and all related matters, at least for the time being. So, where are we going? What do you fancy?"

"I love the opera. Maybe we could…"

Even before I finish he has the iPad fired up again, and is tapping the screen briskly.

"Well, we've got Opera North at the Leeds Grand this evening. How does *Don Giovanni* sound?"

"*Don Giovanni.* Wonderful. But would we be able to get tickets at short notice?"

"James'll sort that. We all have our particular skills, Miss Byrne — sorry, Dr Bryne — and that's his speciality." Still tapping he comes up with more cultural delights. "And tomorrow we've got good old Tennessee Williams at the West Yorkshire Playhouse. *Cat On A Hot Tin Roof.* Would you fancy that?"

I nod, dazed.

"Great. Now what about the ballet? Ah yes, Northern Ballet are doing *The Nutcracker.* But that's in Bradford. We could catch it on Sunday, though, on our way home to Black Combe. Shall I get James to hunt down the tickets for us before he goes home?"

"You want to do all those things, go on all those dates… With me? You want to spend the weekend with me?"

"By the sound of it, it's gonna take us all weekend, sweetheart, at least, to rake through your legendary car wreck. And we'll need lots of light relief. And lots of gentle fucking. Yes?"

I nod, enthusiastic, my face split by a beaming, goofy smile.

"And some not so gentle fucking once I've worked out how to manage your overly masochistic tendencies. So yes, Eva. I want to spend the weekend with you. And then we go back to Black Combe and you take up your previous post as violin tutor. You up for all that?"

"So I'm not fired. Or dumped?"

He shakes his head, smiling. "No, not fired, and not dumped. Okay? Will you stay with me for the weekend?"

"Yes. Yes. Please."

Laughing, he hits the intercom. "James, have you a moment? We need you in here…"

Chapter Two

The weekend was wonderful. I have never enjoyed anything as much as I enjoyed Nathan over those two days. Not just the sex, though that was off the scale. Inventive. Frequent. Intense. But also his humour, his kindness, his light teasing as he drew my story out of me. At the same time he was relentless, leaving me no secrets, nowhere to hide. He has an unerring talent for precision-bombing my least defended areas with his insightful, probing questions, and he extracted the details of my emotional car crash, little by little, gently, firmly, fully.

In deference to my insistent, growling stomach we started at Pizza Express, a few minutes' walk from Nathan's office. We left James with a list of our planned itinerary, chasing up tickets, while we headed for food. I was starving. Absolutely ravenous. Nathan watched, amused, as I guzzled my way through a twelve-inch Hawaiian with extra cheese then waded through a huge slice of chocolate fudge cake. We did ask for two spoons, though, so I told myself that was okay. Not too greedy.

"What a hungry little thing you are, Miss Byrne. You do seem to have worked up quite an appetite. Perhaps I should beat you unconscious more often. Or would you just put on weight?"

I glance up, to catch his wide grin. I smile back, before digging my spoon into the sticky fudge cake once more.

"Not if I get plenty of exercise?"

He laughs out loud at that. "Ah yes, of course, Miss Byrne. Best to keep active. And I can definitely help you with that. Eat up."

Nathan's mobile interrupts our dessert. It's James, his mission accomplished, with instructions for picking up opera tickets at the Leeds Grand box office. The other tickets, for the Playhouse and the ballet in Bradford, will be emailed to Nathan.

"Thanks, James, brilliant job, much appreciated. And thanks for staying late. See you next week. Have a nice weekend." Hanging up, Nathan turns to me, his gorgeous face lit by a sexy smile, his now loose hair flopping around his collar. "We've a couple of hours before we need to be at the theatre. Fancy a walk...by way of keeping active?"

I expected to find myself back in his apartment within minutes, naked, and very thoroughly fucked. So it's come as something of a surprise to be just strolling along the Leeds waterfront, hand in hand, enjoying the balmy warmth of a late summer afternoon. And for once, it's dry. Nathan's still wearing his dark grey suit pants and smart white shirt, meticulously ironed—*I wonder who does that for him?*—but the tie's gone and his jacket is looped over his shoulder. His usual businesslike severity has been switched off with the loosening of his long hair, now brushing his collar, ruffled by the slight breeze. He looks more relaxed, carefree. Softer.

My hair is caught up into a loose plait between my shoulder blades, the best I could do quickly in my hurry to get ready after my shower in Nathan's apartment. I didn't bring a jacket with me when I went down to my 'appointment' at Darke Associates, so I might be cold later. But for now I'm floating. Every few yards I find something interesting to examine and, curious as always, I stop, fish my glasses from my bag and peer at some little touristy plaque commemorating this or that. Nathan just watches me, a strange smile on his mouth. I suspect there's some private joke going on in his head, and it can stay there. I'm doing nothing, saying nothing, asking no questions that might break this mood. Shatter this happy bubble.

I'm happy. Consciously, gloriously happy. Happy now, in this moment. Not, as is more usual for me, in retrospect, looking back, realising afterwards that I was happy *then*. That I used to be happy, whenever. And I also know that my remembered happinesses are few and far between, far too infrequent. I make a mental note to read up on happiness—the psychologists must have done studies. Maybe this is how other people feel. Maybe I could do a course in being happy... How come I never thought of that before? Probably because I didn't realise I wasn't happy, not in the past. I was just getting on with stuff, getting by. Now, I know different.

Apart from a few office types scurrying in the direction of Leeds city station for their Friday evening commute home we have the dock to ourselves. We grab a couple of takeaway Costa lattes and are soon sitting, facing each other across a picnic table on a patio outside the Royal Armouries building. We sip our coffees quietly. Calm. Companionable. Enjoying an interlude of peace and quiet. The perfect opportunity it seems for Nathan to start his campaign to strip me bare.

"So, I'm curious, Eva. 'Profoundly gifted' I think you said... Is that right?" He slants a glance at me before returning to idly stir his latte. He doesn't wait for my answer, not that anything springs immediately to mind. "And I've seen for myself how talented you are. Your academic accomplishments are obvious, your credentials impeccable. A successful academic career as far as I can tell, at some of the best universities in the country." He stops again, glancing at me, waits a moment before continuing, as though expecting me to interrupt. No way that's happening. He shrugs. "And as if that's not enough, you're beautiful too, sexy, fun to be around. You've got it all going on, girl." And now I know he's kidding. Taking the piss. Or got me mixed up with some other sub...

"So, with all that going for you, how come you're scratching out a living temping as a music tutor? How come you'll drive for God knows how many hours in enough rain to drown Noah, arriving in the middle of the fucking night at a perfect stranger's home, to take up a crappy job teaching a little kid to play the violin? And even after I wreck your car and treat you like something I found under my shoe, you still want to stay? In fact, you're desperate to stay. What's all that about, Eva?"

What indeed? The silence stretches between us as I do my usual rabbit-in-headlights impersonation. In truth, there's no explanation I'm prepared to offer. If I understood myself, if I had any real way of coping with the stress of my old life, I wouldn't be sitting here now. His gaze is steady, his words deceptively gentle. I am in no doubt about the steel beneath and I dread the pressure he could exert if he chose. But on this occasion he's content, it would seem, to let all that lie for now. It's registered, recorded. To be continued. He sips his coffee, regarding me intently over the rim.

"Your coffee's going cold." He shoves my paper cup towards me and I pick it up obediently. The subject's safely dropped and we can both enjoy our coffee, back to companionable silence again.

Then, "So, car crash, is it? What did you crash in to Eva?"

Whoa! Where did that come from? Caught off balance again I splash hot coffee onto my hand. Taking my palm in both of his he blows on my skin to cool it, then kisses each of my fingers gently, in turn. "Tell me, Eva. What's in that pile of wreckage of yours?"

Sensing I won't be let off the hook this time, I retreat immediately into my default position of defensiveness and denial. "It doesn't matter. I don't know where to start. Lots of things. Nothing important. It can wait." I'm reluctant, shy suddenly, and desperate to hide. I don't want to spoil this lovely evening, burst my happiness bubble, intrude on it with talk of my screwed up past.

"All right. Shall I start then?" At my look of surprise he smiles, goes on. "Shall I tell you what I know about you already? What I've seen? You can tell me if I'm right. Okay?"

I nod. "Okay," I whisper, grateful that he's still holding my hand, stroking it lightly. I can concentrate on watching his hands on mine and not have to meet his eyes.

"I think you like to be looked after, pampered. You like having your hair dried, or your back washed in the shower, but I think you're not used to it. Am I right so far?"

That's not what I expected him to home in on, but it seems safe enough, I've got worse secrets. I nod. He goes on. My sense of safety evaporates. Precision bombing.

"But you jumped two feet in the air when I wrapped the towel round your hair, that first morning, in Grace's kitchen. I thought you were going to bolt. I forced you back into your chair. Do you remember?"

Christ, yes!

He continues, his tone deceptively low as his words hit their target. Dead centre. "You were—scared? Were you scared of me even then, Eva?"

I can only stare at our hands, my mind whirling as I desperately grope around for words, for an answer, any response that might deflect him. He's not having it. Gently squeezing my hand he lifts it again, kisses it, before reaching across the table. Taking my chin in his fingers he tips my face up, forcing eye contact. His dark chocolate eyes are soft, kind, compassionate. "Talk to me, Eva. I'm listening. Were you scared of me?"

I take a deep breath, and jump off the cliff.

"Not you. Well yes, you. But generally, not just because of the towel."

"You were scared of me? And you hadn't even seen my whip collection then."

I laugh, appreciating his dark humour. "I'm scared of everyone. Well, all men. Please don't take it personally. No offence."

"None taken, love. And now? Are you still scared? Of me? Or of all men?"

Again studying our linked hands my reply is quiet, but stronger, more certain. It's getting easier to share this stuff. With Nathan.

"Men—yes, probably. I think I always will be. I'm sort of—inhibited—I suppose you'd say. I'm very shy. Usually."

"I know you're shy, love. You blush a lot. It's one of the things I first noticed about you. Because you're so pretty when you blush, it makes me hard, makes me want to fuck you. And it brings out the worst in me, I'm afraid. It makes me want to talk very dirty to you just to make you blush more."

I look up, startled at the unexpected sexual compliment. I feel myself starting to become wet, just anticipating the aforementioned fucking. He's not done, though.

"But we were talking about being scared as well as shy. Are you still scared of me?"

I think for a moment, then answer him honestly, "Yes, definitely. Sometimes. And sometimes not. And sometimes there are times when you scare me so much I think I might just die of it. Is it possible to die of fear?"

"No. Maybe. I'm not sure. You won't die of fear, though, not with me. Because you know, in your heart you do know, I won't ever hurt you. Do you believe that, Eva?"

"Yes," I whisper, so softly he has to lean forward to catch it. But he does. Now he knows. I do trust him. And now I know it too.

Suddenly something else bursts out, before even I know what I'm about to say. "I don't like to be touched. No one ever touches me. I don't allow it." I pull my hand away, to prove my point. I stare at the table top, half expecting to see my words wriggling there, like black, ugly worms.

I hate worms—just one more of my many, many hang-ups. And I hate no longer being able to keep my secrets safe. My dam is breaking. I'm terrified of what might escape next.

Unruffled, Nathan reaches across, takes my hand back. Calm. Gentle. Firm. "I've done nothing but touch you since the night you arrived at my house, Eva. And I know for a fact you liked it. Mostly."

I babble. In my bewildered, chaotic state I just pour out my confusion. Tip more wriggling worms onto the table. Let him sort them out. Make sense of it if he can.

"But that's just it. Only you. No one else. Ever. Not even my mum. But I sat still and let you dry my hair. And I let you kiss me, on the lane when we were stargazing." I am looking at him now, wide-eyed, baffled. His head cocked to one side he listens, saying nothing, letting me continue. "It felt different when you did it. It was nice. It felt right. I think. Sort of. I was so surprised, so delighted, I don't know how it happened. I just wanted more. I wanted you to never stop touching me." Embarrassed, I fall silent.

"Is that why you agreed to come to Leeds with me then? To let me touch you some more?"

It would be easy to just agree, leave it at that, but my relentless honesty is in full flow now. I want to tell it like it is. "No. I agreed because you had me flat on my back, topless, on Mrs Richardson's kitchen table. I was so close to my first orgasm, I needed it, so much. And you kept on at me. Bullying me. I was desperate, scared you'd just stop if I didn't do as you wanted, just dump me, leave me hanging." My voice faltering, I stumble on, whispering now, uncomfortable and vulnerable. "I've been close before, once or twice, but never managed to…you know…finish."

He lifts my hand, kisses it, quirks his lip, has the grace to look slightly awkward as he regards me over my clenched knuckles. "Your first orgasm? I didn't realise that. I wasn't very kind to you, was I?"

I shake my head, my face flaming with humiliation. No doubt he'll notice me blushing again, be keen to fuck me at his earliest convenience. That should be nice…

"And I was none too gentle the first time I fucked you either. I didn't realise then that you were a virgin, but all the same, I could have been more considerate." That wry smile is back, his lip curling up at one side as he grins at me wickedly. "There was no real need to tie you up, I suppose, thinking back. You did say you weren't going anywhere."

More gallows humour, just at the right time to lighten my mood, restore my confidence. And re-establish that easy rapport from earlier. I grin back at him. "Well that's just you, isn't it, Nathan? I bet you can't even get it up without the handcuffs and ropes. Without all your fancy props."

He laughs out loud, his face split by a huge grin, broad, fun-filled. "Miss Byrne, are you angling for some hands-free fucking? You've only to ask, I'd be delighted to demonstrate."

"Thank you, that will be most pleasant, I'm sure."

"Pleasant! Miss Byrne, have a care for my ego. Your sweet little bottom is going to pay for that last remark. But first, we've an opera to catch. Time to go."

As suddenly as it started the navel-gazing is over. For now. He throws both our empty Costa cups in a bin before grabbing my hand tightly and pulling me to my feet. Draping an arm round my shoulders, he kisses me soundly before tugging me off down the waterfront towards Leeds city centre.

* * * *

The opera was wonderful. James did well for us. We had seats in the circle, near the front. *Don Giovanni* has always been one of my absolute favourite operas, one of Mozart's finest pieces. The performance was exquisite, passionate, humorous and engaging. And in the original Italian, one of my favourite languages. My Italian is fluent. I spent most of the three hours with tears streaming down my face. Opera invariably moves me, the passion, the musicality, the drama. And with my own Dom Juan sitting next to me, just waiting to seduce me again the first opportunity he gets, I could empathise with the infatuated conquests and victims. And I'm sure my mother would have found much common cause with the vengeful families.

Afterwards we caught a late supper at an old bank, now converted into a trendy wine and noodle bar. We giggled over chopsticks and chicken chow mein, washed down with a crisp, chilled Chardonnay. Then we strolled back across the dark, deserted city centre, Nathan's jacket over my shoulders, holding hands again and snogging like teenagers in shop doorways. Me making up for lost time and missed opportunities in my far-from-misspent youth, and Nathan just having fun.

Nathan kept dropping change in the outstretched hands of homeless people, wrapped in an assortment of tatty coats and pullovers, as often as not accompanied by skinny little mongrel dogs on bits of string. And as often as not we found ourselves sharing the doorways with them. He was very generous, much to my surprise really. My mother always warned me not to give money to beggars. "It just encourages them," she'd say, and in London I always scuttle past, not meeting their eyes.

"Maybe some of them are trying it on, scroungers like you say, but I always think you'd have to be pretty bloody desperate to want to make your living that way," Nathan says, in answer to my query. "I'm just glad I've somewhere to go tonight. And a beautiful woman to go there with." He hugs me closer. "If one or two of them have cheated me, I'll survive it. I think most are genuine, though, and I know that life can be pretty crap."

Well yes, no argument out of me on that one. But looking into the empty, hopeless eyes of the Leeds vagrants I think there's crap, which is me a lot of the time, and there's absolute total shit. I hug Nathan back.

Then, another of his mercurial changes of mood. "So tell me, Miss Byrne. Sorry, Dr Byrne — do you still have those cute little lacy knickers on?"

"What? No!"

"No knickers? Dr Byrne, you shock me."

"Idiot. No. Different ones. These are pink."

"Ah, gorgeous. I do like you in pink, sets off your gorgeous red hair. All your red hair. Everywhere. Which reminds me, I intend to remove it for you. I want you nice and smooth."

"Remove it? Remove what?"

"Your hair. Your lovely red pubic hair, Miss Byrne."

"What, tonight? Why? How?"

"Not tonight. Best not to get too near your sweet little fanny with sharp implements after half a bottle of wine. Might damage something precious. Tomorrow, though."

I'm puzzled, but what the hell? "Okay, if you want to. But why?"

"Because it's so pretty afterwards. And so erotic while I'm doing it. And when I say I want you naked, Eva, I mean properly naked."

"How will you do it?" I think of the sharp implements. "Will you shave it off?"

"No. Too bristly and scratchy. I'm thinking a nice wax job. Smarts a bit, but very effective."

"Waxing! There! You're joking. What about cream?"

"We haven't known each other that long, I do realise, but have you ever known me to joke about what I intend to do to you, Miss Byrne?"

"Er, no…"

"No. And cream's not safe to use on genitals. Must think of your health and safety, Dr Byrne. So a Brazilian wax then? Tomorrow. Agreed?"

It does indeed seem to be settled. "I… I suppose so. Does it hurt a lot?"

"Not too much. If I do it quick. And I've done much, much worse to you already. You'll be fine with this. Don't look so worried." His hand on my bum takes my mind off tomorrow's events, reminding me there are more immediate matters to attend to.

We continue to stroll in the direction of the waterfront once more, and arrive back at Nathan's apartment around midnight. As soon as the lift doors close he is on me, kissing me, exploring my mouth with his tongue while pulling my shirt from my pants. Deftly undoing the buttons, before I know it he has my hands caught behind my back, tangled in the sleeves. Lifting his head to glance appreciatively at my new, pink lacy bra he cups my breasts, squeezing gently, lowering his head to kiss the mounds visible above the lace. "So sweet, Eva, so pretty," he breathes, and I vaguely wonder if he means my underwear or my body. Who cares? He flicks open the front fastening of my bra to bare my breasts for his ministrations. With his mouth and clever fingers my nipples are brought to swollen, aching hardness before the lift arrives at the penthouse, and the doors glide open.

It's only when he takes my elbow to tug me forward into the apartment that I realise my hands are effectively tied behind my back, still caught up in my discarded blouse. I wriggle, trying to free myself so I can kiss him back, hold him, but he smiles down, knowingly. I realise he's done this on purpose. And that he won't free me until he's good and ready. After dropping a light kiss on my lips, he opens the door to the apartment and gestures for me to enter before him.

Once inside, Nathan leaves me standing, topless, in the middle of his living room as he goes over to the fridge. Pulling out a chilled bottle of wine he quickly uncorks it and pours one glass. Strolling back towards me, the glass in his right hand, his eyes are on my breasts, admiring, lustful. I realise my usual inhibitions might be diminishing, but have not yet disappeared as I wish I was better endowed, curvier. Nathan doesn't seem to mind, though, as with his free left hand he cups and massages my breast whilst he reaches with his right hand, still holding the glass, to curl it behind my neck. He pulls me close, kissing my ear, nibbling the lobe before dropping his face to my neck.

"Christ, Eva, you are a beautiful sight. Perfect. Exquisite." He kisses me again before sipping the wine.

"Would you like a drink, Eva?"

I nod. "Yes, please. But you'll have to hold the glass." I roll my shoulders to indicate my bound hands.

He smiles. "Ah, yes, anything to be of service, Miss Byrne."

He lifts the glass to my lips, tipping a little of the crisp chilled liquid into my mouth before immediately following it in with his tongue, tasting the wine before it disappears down my throat.

"I do like to share, Miss Byrne," he murmurs before taking another sip himself. This time, though, he catches my mouth in a deep, open-mouthed kiss, letting the liquid pour from his tongue onto mine. It feels sensuous, intimate, delicious. I moan, swallow quickly in surprised contentment.

"More, Miss Byrne?" he asks softly, his dark eyes shining inches from mine.

"Yes. Yes, please."

Several wine-kisses later he is back to nuzzling my neck. "This is a good wine, don't you agree, Miss Byrne? Chilled enough for you?"

"Yes, yes, I think so." *Who cares how cold it is? Just keep on kissing me with it...*

In the next moment I suddenly do care. Very much.

"Ah, that's good then. Because I intend to drink it off your nipples, Miss Byrne. But first, I need your pretty little tits to be thrust out at me, just a little more."

Before I can respond, or even think straight, he has placed the wine glass on a side table and turned me around. Taking the straps of my bra still loosely hanging from my arms, he uses them to form loops around my elbows. With a few deft twists he has tightened the loops to pull my elbows closer together, forcing my shoulders back and my breasts out. The position is slightly painful, stretching the muscles across my chest. Turning me around to face him again he glances down.

"Much better, Miss Byrne. Are you comfortable?"

"It feels a little…tight."

"Good. You'll get used to it." Without further conversation he undoes the button and zip on my chinos, before pushing the trousers down over my hips to pool at my feet. My pink lace knickers soon follow and I am naked again, since my blouse and bra can hardly count.

"Kneel down, Miss Byrne." I comply, and he drops to sit next to me, still fully clothed. I shiver involuntarily as his hands skim my breasts, my nipples. After reaching for the wine glass, he places it on the floor beside us, dipping his finger into it. He smears the wine across my left nipple, admiring his handiwork before repeating the action with my right nipple. Then he bends his head, takes my left nipple in his mouth and sucks, hard. I gasp, the sensation almost painful in its intensity as my defenceless breasts are pushed forward for his attention. My right nipple gets the same treatment, and this time I gasp in pleasure/pain as he bites the swollen tip, not hard but enough for me to feel it. Really feel it.

"Ah, Nathan, please…" I throw my head back and I realise he is supporting my weight, one arm behind me, holding me still for his mouth to do its work.

"Nathan, please what? What do you want, Eva?" His voice is low, soft. "More of this? More wine, Eva?"

This time he pours the liquid directly onto my throbbing nipples, smiling as I wince at the chill. Swirling his tongue around my breasts he licks the wine off, grazing me with his teeth before taking my right nipple firmly between his lips and flicking it hard with his tongue. He then treats my left nipple to the same tender care. The sensation is so intense that I try instinctively to pull back, but his arm tightens behind me, holding me in place.

"I think the wine is getting warm, Eva. Can't have that."

Releasing me he is suddenly on his feet, walking away. Confused, I watch him open the fridge again, but this time he's in the freezer compartment. With a sharp snap he has dislodged a handful of ice cubes from a tray into another wine glass. He brings the ice back to me, rattling the cubes inside the glass. He drops back down to sit beside me once more.

"For chilling the wine," he says, dropping a cube into the crisp sparkling liquid. "And for cooling you down. Are you hot, Dr Byrne?"

"I…I'm not sure…maybe."

"Yes, I think you may be too." Slipping an ice cube into his mouth he leans in, kissing me and gently transferring it to my mouth. "Suck, Dr Byrne. Is that good?" I nod, and he smiles, "Enough? Okay, my turn…" He leans in again, taking the ice cube back into his mouth. Holding it between his lips he rolls his tongue over it for a minute or two, all the while gazing at me and rolling first one nipple then the other between his finger and thumb. He is gentle now, his touch light, teasing. I want more, more firmness, more pressure.

With a quick smile he again transfers the ice cube to my mouth before dropping his head to take my nipple between his chilled lips. The sensation is—exquisite. Cool, soothing, promising more.

This time he puts the wine glass in front of my mouth. "Open, Miss Byrne. Drop it." I drop the now much depleted ice cube into the liquid with a plop. He takes a sip of the wine before lifting it to my mouth, offering me another drink. I sip, swallow, wait.

After putting the glass behind him he takes another ice cube, places it in his mouth, held firmly between his teeth. I open my mouth, expecting to receive it, but this time he dips his head, touching the ice directly onto my swollen, hard nipple. I shriek, and he tightens his hold as I struggle to escape the sudden shock, the intense sensation shooting through me. My nipple swells even further, if that were possible, throbbing, hard. Holding me immobile he moves to the other breast, treating that engorged tip to the same icy caress, drawing the ice across and around until that nipple too has swelled, hardened. Only when I stop struggling, lying still under his chilly mouth, does he reach out for another ice cube, taking that in his fingers and picking up the action again with my other nipple. I lie still now, breathing hard, panting even as he rubs the ice slowly over both my nipples. After a few moments I realise that the cold is actually numbing the sensations. It's no longer especially cold. Or painful. It feels strange, other-worldly, as though I am detached from what he is doing to my body. I am aware when he drops the ice cube back into the glass and takes my nipple between his finger and thumb, squeezing, pinching tight. I can feel the pressure, but no pain through my frozen flesh.

Sitting up he slips his hand into his trouser pocket, pulling something out. Something small, something purple, something very, very familiar.

The sweet little nipple clamps lie across his palm. He shows them to me, not speaking, his eyebrow lifted, asking wordlessly for permission. I gulp. Then I nod, settling back to let him do whatever needs to be done.

"You'll hardly feel this at first, and I won't make them too tight, this time." He quickly slips a small crocodile clip around each of my nipples, first the left, then the right, releasing the springs slowly, carefully, letting the jaws close around me. He glances up, making sure I'm okay, that I can handle this. And, I suspect, to make sure I know I'm getting let off lightly, no doubt because he now thinks I'm soft after I passed out on him this morning, that I need special care. Maybe I do.

"And next time I may not use the ice to deaden the initial pain. As the sensation comes back into your nipples over the next couple of minutes it will hurt, but it'll build more slowly so you can get used to it." He is gently rubbing each of my swollen nipples with his thumbs, watching me carefully, and knows the instant the sensation starts to bite. I jerk, but he continues to stroke me, gently bringing the sensations back. And God what sensations. The tight, pinching, squeezing pressure is so intense I whimper, gritting my teeth as the pain builds, radiating out through my body.

"Nathan, it hurts, please, I can't..." I start to plead, wondering if I should be screaming 'red' at the top of my voice.

"Hang on in there, sweetheart, ride the pain. Get past it." His voice is gentle, soothing, his fingers light as he continues to massage my throbbing, smarting nipples. After what seems an eternity, but in reality is only a couple of minutes, the pain starts to blend into the pleasure. I can feel the clamps, and the weighted 'bullets' suspended from them, and every time I move the sensation of tugging sweeps through me. I realise Nathan has sat back, dropped his hands, and is now watching me as I sit, still at last, calm at last, the nipple clamps firmly gripping me.

"You okay, angel?" he asks, and I smile, close my eyes, nod slowly.

I feel the slight tug as he lifts the bullets, taking their weight before dropping them again. My eyes shoot open and I jerk forward, give a sharp little cry as the sudden vibration streaks through my nipples like an electric current, shooting straight to my groin as the sensations all meet there. I feel desire pool, clench, pulsing, throbbing. I am moaning, my hips gyrating as I strive for orgasm, just out of reach, elusive, rushing through me then dancing away.

Nathan watches me for a few moments before taking pity. Pulling me onto his lap, my back against his chest, he kisses my shoulders, his hands taking the weight of my sensitised breasts though not the weight of the vibrating bullets hanging from my nipples. He gives a little shake, the bullets swing, tug. I gasp as the sensation shifts, lances through me again. He shifts behind me, under me, and I feel the large, hard shaft of his erection beneath my buttocks, pressing upwards into me. Only his trousers stop him from penetrating me, and I wriggle against him, wanting him. Then his hand drops lower, between my legs as he slides his finger through my curls to the slick, hot flesh beyond.

"Open your legs wide, Eva," he whispers into my ear. "Wider. Let me touch you."

I do, gladly, gratefully, as he strokes my clitoris with his clever fingers. At first he is gentle, teasing, featherlight in his touch, but as my arousal grows he strokes me more firmly, pressing harder, more insistent. "Is this good, Eva? Is this how you like it?"

"Yes. Yes. Oh, that's fabulous. Fabulous."

"More? Would you like more, Eva?"

"Please, yes. Please don't stop. I just need..."

"Is this what you need, angel?" He continues to circle and rub my clit with his thumb as he slips two fingers deep inside me, and with a final scream I am gone. The clenching, clutching convulsions of my powerful orgasm grip me, grip him as the walls of my vagina squeeze around his fingers, still moving inside me to draw out the final waves of pleasure.

At last I am still, lying back against him, his arms around me, one hand across my stomach, the other still between my legs, still lightly caressing me. Soothing me, reassuring me as my senses return. He kisses my ear, nuzzling his face in my hair, still loosely plaited, tendrils falling free around my face.

I feel the release of pressure on my nipples as he opens the clamps, removing them gently. He rolls the still painful tips between his fingers, encouraging the circulation back to normal. "Is this sore, love?" he asks as I wince under his hands.

"Yes, a little. But it was wonderful. Thank you. And thank you for the ice, at the beginning. I don't think I could have managed it otherwise." I twist my head to look up at him, into his deep, chocolate eyes. He is smiling, his expression tender, caring.

"I told you, Eva, that I'd stretch you, push you to your limits. But that I'd never hurt you more than you can bear. You needed the ice, this time. But next time, who knows?" His grin mischievous now, he leans down, plants a quick kiss on my lips, before pulling me upright in front of him. With a few deft tugs my hands and arms are free, and I realise how much they are aching as I pull them stiffly in front of me, rubbing my joints to get them loose and moving again. Nathan stands, pulling me to my feet. I notice with surprise that he is still fully dressed, and open my mouth to comment on that as he sweeps me into his arms. I decide to cling on instead as he strides across the room and through the door to his bedroom. He drops me in the middle of his huge bed, standing over me as he wastes no time in shedding his clothes. The shirt goes first, and my mouth waters as I admire his sculpted chest and defined abdomen muscles. His trousers are next, then his shorts, and his powerful, huge erection juts out at me.

The head of his penis is slick, a bead of moisture on the end. I reach out to touch it, to smooth it across the tip with my thumb as he so recently rubbed my nipples. With my other hand I cup his balls, heavy, taut, moving in my palm. I shift, intending to take him in my mouth, but this time he stops me, coming onto the bed to kneel over me, pressing me back against the duvet. His hands behind my knees, he parts my legs, positioning himself between them. He pushes my knees upwards, holding them either side of my chest, raising me up for better access, better entrance.

"Just a little gentle fucking now, Eva, does that sound nice to you?"

"Yes, that sounds very nice. But not too gentle. Please."

"Anything to oblige." He enters me quick, hard, deep. I feel his cock hit my cervix as his balls slap against my bottom. He is huge, wide. I feel my inner walls stretch to accommodate him, but there is no pain this time. He gives me a moment to adjust before starting to thrust. Slow at first, pulling right back almost out of me, then deeply, smoothly plunging fully into me once more, right to the hilt. I groan, writhe under him. He shifts slightly to get the perfect angle to hit that certain spot, and sets up a rhythm. I moan with pleasure as he strokes me smoothly, the friction delicious and delicate against my vagina, and the now familiar first tug of orgasm drifts across me. I squeeze him, crossing my ankles behind his waist to pull him farther in. His hands now free, he slips one between us to lay his thumb over my clit, every thrust causing the sensitive little bud to scrape against him. Quickly the pleasure builds until I shatter, crying out as I clench and convulse again, and he stiffens above me, holding himself very still for the few seconds it takes for my orgasm to pass.

When I am still again, my legs flat on the bed beneath him, he drops down, his weight on me, and takes my face between his palms. He kisses me, long and deep, not moving again, not yet, but still huge and hard inside me. After a few moments he pushes himself up, placing his knees under my bottom so I am lifted up, my hips draped across his thighs. He looks down at that spot where we are joined, then back into my eyes.

"So sweet, Eva, so fucking gorgeous." Then with his hands resting in my groin he uses both his thumbs to stimulate my clit again, running them alternately along the swollen nub, from my entrance, now stretched fully open by his cock planted deep within me, towards the front. Continuously stroking, the pleasure is absolutely overwhelming. The intimacy of the gesture, the tender, caring, gentle caress so sweet I feel tears behind my closed eyelids.

In that moment I know for sure that I can, will, do love this man.

I'm so tired now I can hardly move in response to the waves of pure pleasure washing through me, but I know I don't need to. He knows. He is watching me, and as my climax again rushes towards me he increases the pressure enough to send me spinning away once more, floating, shaking, convulsing until eventually I lie still. One very satisfied, very contented little sub.

Leaning over me once more, with a couple of sharp, hard thrusts, and a muffled curse, he is done. I feel his hot sperm shoot deep inside me, as the shudders ripple through his tight, hard muscles, the veins on his arms standing out as he strains against me, inside me. Then suddenly his arms give way and he drops onto me. I expect his full weight to pin me to the bed again, but at the last moment he rolls, taking me with him as he did before, that first time when I cried all over his chest, and once more I land on top. He is still inside me, but only just as his erection slips away. I shift slightly, and we are separated. Which does seem a pity.

"You okay, sweetheart? Not too rough?"

"I'm fine. Absolutely wonderful. And the fucking was wonderful too."

I wonder if, when, I should tell him I love him. Is that suitable conversation from a sub to her Dom? Probably not.

Shit!

Chapter Three

We slept late on Saturday morning. Well I did, certainly. Sex with Nathan, indeed everything with Nathan, is wonderful. Sensual, intense, all-consuming and absolutely exhausting. I have felt drained each time, and slept like a log.

It is bright daylight when I awake, the summer sunshine streaming into the room, warm and golden. Or maybe that's just me. I squint over at the clock. Ten fifteen. I can hear Nathan moving about in the kitchen, the splash of water and clink of crockery suggesting the possibility of coffee on its way. On that optimistic thought I roll over, snuggle happily back down into the duvet and wait, hugging my tummy in excitement as I rewind through yesterday's events. The trauma of yesterday morning, the shock and tension of the afternoon's interview in Nathan's office and the sweetness of the evening, topped off by the most incredible lovemaking. Although Nathan would never call it that. To him it's always fucking. Sometimes gentle, sometimes not at all gentle, but always fucking. A Dom fucking his sub. Simple.

But this sub's in love. Or thinks she is. Except, hell, how would I know, really? I've no solid frame of reference for this, and given what we've been getting up to, who could I ask? My mother? Normally I might talk to her. Maybe. But I can just imagine the conversation. 'Mum, there's this guy I've met and been sleeping with. He's a dab hand with a whip and can do amazing things with nipple clamps. And I think I might be in love with him. Oh, and yes, I'm not a virgin anymore...' I think not!

I have a strong suspicion this is not going to turn out to be simple at all, especially when Nathan gets wind of how I feel. Yesterday I was afraid he'd dump me for being a freak. Today I think he'll quite probably dump me for being in love.

Shit indeed.

"Coffee, croissants, paracetamol and a nice long, hot bath. In that order." I hear the clink of cups as Nathan plants a tray on the end of the bed and sits beside me.

Paracetamol?

I roll over onto my back, nervous suddenly as he peels back the duvet to reveal my breasts. He runs his fingers from my shoulder, down over my breasts to circle my nipples, then onto my tummy, quirking one sexy eyebrow, his smile reassuring, familiar, intimate. His touch feels natural, safe. I arch into it. But apparently just now he has different ideas.

"Sit up, time for breakfast." He pulls me up briskly, propping pillows behind me and scrambles onto the bed himself to lounge alongside me. He has on his boxers but that's all, his long muscled legs stretched out on top of the duvet. I make a mental note to ask him how he keeps his superb body in shape, but first things first...

"Who's the paracetamol for? Got a headache?"

"It's for you, sassy lady. You'll be glad of it."

He grabs a croissant, tears off a chunk and shoves it into his mouth, washing it down with coffee before turning to me.

"You've got your first Brazilian wax coming up. It is your first, I assume…?"

I nod slowly, wishing I'd paid more attention yesterday.

"Well then, that's gonna hurt. Probably. The painkillers will help, though, and if you take them before your bath they'll have time to kick in. So, eat up, and get those tits under control, or I'll fuck you now until you faint again."

I pull up the duvet, instinctively squeezing my legs shut at the thought of the upcoming wax job, but he laughs and tugs it down again. "Relax, Eva. It's a lovely view and very tempting, but I'll manage to control myself. Well, for a few more minutes anyway. Don't want you to starve. So eat."

"Right, sir," I mutter, "Straight away, sir," reaching for a croissant.

"You were right, you do catch on fast." He chuckles, and takes another glug of his coffee.

If only he knew.

"I'll run you a bath. Help to soften you up for your wax job." And he is gone, disappearing out of the door again, presumably to some house bathroom as the en suite is only blessed with a shower. A jumbo-sized power shower plenty big enough for two, but no bath. The sound of running water from somewhere out in the apartment tells me the morning's fun and games are on.

I eat my croissants leisurely, and sip my coffee. Then pour myself another cup. Let him wait. I know full well he'll come and get me when he's ready.

As the minutes tick by and no Nathan reappears I begin to get curious, especially when the sound of running water stops. I slide out of bed and nip in the en suite to use the loo. Then, still not quite sufficiently uninhibited to walk around his apartment naked, I slip into Nathan's discarded shirt from last night and go looking for him.

I take my time. This is the first chance I've had to wander round, explore this place where Nathan lives for half his life. And on closer examination it really is very impressive. The airy lounge area opens into a dining space, which then extends off into the kitchen. Like at Black Combe, everything is state of the art, expensive, classy. From the black granite worktops to the glistening halogen hob, from the huge flat-screen TV to the Bose sound system, everything is top quality, designed for comfort, and for luxury. The leather sofas facing each other across the lounge, the beautiful oak dining table and matching carver chairs, the Aubusson rugs scattered around the hardwood floor, all speak of taste and perfection. There is modern art on the walls, not an area I know much about, but I am sure Nathan has chosen well. The place is pristine, spotless. He obviously employs someone to look after it all for him—I can't somehow imagine the sexy Mr Darke flitting round with a duster.

Small personal items are placed around the space—a photo of Rosie on top of an upturned beer crate—very trendy, a Leeds United supporters' scarf dangling over the back of one of the dining chairs and a guitar case leaning against the kitchen worktop.

I can't help myself, I have to open it, have a look at the instrument inside. I lift it out carefully, a Fender acoustic guitar, not top of the range but certainly sweet enough. I dig around in the case for a plectrum and, finding one, settle on the arm of the sofa, the instrument across my knees, and strum gently. I listen for the tone, absently twisting the tuning pegs on the neck to get the perfect sound. I may be making my living as a violinist just now, but in fact my best efforts are on the piano, which I play to concert standard. There really isn't any musical instrument, though, that I can't get a decent tune out of within a few minutes of experimenting and I reckon this sweet little Fender will be no exception. I remember myself in time — it's rude to just pick up someone else's instrument and play without permission. I'd go spare if anyone messed with my violin. Regretfully I place the Fender back in the case and prop it up against the worktop where I found it. And hope he hasn't heard me.

I stroll over to the floor to ceiling picture window and realise it is actually a patio door, leading to a stunning rooftop terrace and garden. There is outdoor furniture, ornamental trees in huge pots and even two life size statues of sheep, grazing on a small patch of grass. Real grass? Looks like it. And all with breathtaking views over the Leeds city skyline. Private, secluded, Nathan's own little oasis in the heart of the city.

But for all the high-end interior design and stunning location this place is not a show home. It's a place that is lived in, played in, enjoyed. The overall effect is one of invitation, of welcome. It's not quite Black Combe, but still, I love it.

I really do need to find him now, though, before he gets irritated and comes looking for me. My instincts tell me I should avoid irritating him if I can. Glancing around there are only two other doors Nathan could have gone through. I know which is his bedroom, obviously, and which is the guest room I used on Thursday, when I was getting ready for the awards dinner. I try the first possibility and find myself looking into a small home office. A quick glance tells me, not surprisingly, that it's fully fitted out, dominated by a mean-looking desktop computer with a huge screen — I remember that Nathan is an architect so probably uses CAD. He also has a traditional drawing board under a large window, no doubt catching the best natural light.

I step back, closing the door softly, and turn to the last remaining possibility. I turn the knob and open the door, peeping inside. Wow! This is it. This is the most beautiful, luxurious bathroom I have ever seen. I step inside, close the door and lean back against it, taking in the sight.

The spacious room, tiled in black with shiny brass fittings, is dominated by a huge bath. The bath is deep and wide, and looks to be made of wood. It's full to the brim, topped by a layer of rich bubbles, and Nathan is lounging at one end, his arm slung casually over the side, a glass of what looks to be orange juice in his other hand, watching me quietly.

"You took your time, Miss Byrne. I guess you've been exploring?"

"Yes. I had a look around. Is that okay? I didn't mean to pry or anything, it's just that this place is... Well — wow, look at all this!" I step forward, eyes wide and open-mouthed, turning slowly to take it all in. The heated towel rail, the piles of fluffy cream-coloured towels, another multi-jet shower behind a teak semi-screen, another loo discreetly tucked away behind more teak. A double sink unit set into a polished teak vanity, the shelf above sporting such mundane necessities as toothbrushes, toothpaste, soap and a flannel.

But the bath, the magnificent bath, is centre stage, free-standing in the middle of the room, with a small step in front of it. There are shelves at the rim level, to two sides, where Nathan has placed a jug of orange juice, a half bottle of champagne, opened, a small bottle of chilled water and two small white tablets in a tiny porcelain dish. No candles, but the lighting is soft, seductive. And the scent of pine and forest fills the steamy air.

He smiles, obviously cool with my curiosity. "No problem, you're welcome. I'll do the grand tour for you later. And you can demonstrate your prowess on my guitar again. Another of your private concerts, perhaps?" *Oh hell, he did hear then…*

"But now, come and join me, Miss Byrne," he says, still smiling softly, but the thread of steel is back.

"Is this thing made of wood?" I ask, incredulous. I've never heard of a wooden bath. "Won't it leak?"

"Yes. And no, it won't leak. It's seasoned, treated teak. Built for warmth. And comfort. And pleasure, Miss Byrne. So get in. Now, please."

I catch the warning note in his tone, but find I'm not quite so easily cowed anymore. With an impressive show of defiant bravado, somewhat undermined by my need to use the step to clamber up onto the bath I sit on the edge, looking down at him. I'm still wearing his shirt and making no move yet to undress for him.

His gaze hardening as he notes my show of defiance, he takes a sip of his orange juice. And offers me one last chance. "My shirt looks much better on you than it did on me, Miss Byrne, but take it off now, please."

I turn to dangle my bare legs and feet in the tub, still perched on the edge, watching him, waiting, defying.

Goading him. Sooner or later Nathan's Dom persona is going to surface, and recklessly I rather think I'd like to see that now.

Nathan does not disappoint. Discreetly setting his drink down, he gives me probably a full five seconds more to comply with his instructions before he lunges for me, grabs me and pulls me in, shirt as well. The bath is about three feet deep and I am under the water, struggling in his strong arms for the few moments he takes to pull me, gasping, to the surface. Coughing and spluttering I fight to push my masses of wet hair away from my face and glare at him, spitting outrage and accusation.

He is unmoved. "The shirt, Miss Byrne. Or do I need to duck you again?"

"The list said no drowning." I snarl at him, affronted by this breach of our agreement. How dare he!

"You'll know soon enough if I decide to drown you. The list also said obedience. Immediate, no arguing. So, for the last time, Miss Byrne…?"

I know when not to push it—my Dom is back in full force, and scary as hell. "Okay, okay," I mutter, starting to unbutton the shirt but struggling with the wet fabric. Apart from holding me by the waist to steady me and keep me afloat he doesn't help, just watches me fiddling with the buttons until eventually the shirt floats free. He grabs it and tosses it out onto the tiled floor before taking a long look up and down my body. Appreciating, admiring, owning…?

"Much better. Now, your medication, Miss Byrne." He passes me the porcelain dish and, docile now, I scoop the two painkillers into my hand, tossing them into my mouth as he passes me the bottle of water to wash them down. I screw up my face at the bitter taste.

"They'll do you good. Now, do you want a more pleasant drink as a chaser? Juice? Buck's Fizz?"

"Er, what are you having?"

"Bit early for me to hit the hard stuff. And anyway I want to keep a clear head, and you'll be glad of that soon enough when I get to work on your sweet little body. But you? If you want a drink that's fine. Might even steady your nerves."

I'm tempted, but probably best not. "Just juice, please. I think I'll keep my head clear too."

His lopsided grin is his only response as he pours me a glass of orange. Then turning me easily in the water he pulls me against him, my back up against his hard chest. He reaches round me to hand me the glass, then lays back, his arm loosely around my middle. He picks up his own glass again, takes a leisurely sip. Then, putting his drink down on the shelf alongside his head he reaches out, picks up a small remote control. Pointing it at a wall-mounted sensor on the opposite wall he presses a button, and a moment later the room is bathed in sound. The wonderful, melodious sound of classical guitar. I feel myself relax against him, immediately enchanted by the music. I love classical guitar, play a bit myself but not in this class. Nevertheless, I can appreciate the naked acoustic beauty of Milos Karadaglic's *Latino*.

"Like that?" He murmurs the question softly against my ear. I nod contentedly. "Mmm, thought you might. And later you'll play for me again?" It could be a question, a request, or perhaps an instruction. I decide to test the water, so to speak.

"Maybe," I respond. "Depends how much I dislike you after the waxing." No harm in flexing my own muscles, such as they are. Occasionally. And it seems I've got away with it. This time. No further words required, I lie back, luxuriating in the warm, scented water, lulled by the delicate, evocative, intricate strains of Milos' exquisite skill.

Nathan stretches out his arm again and flicks a switch. Suddenly the water explodes into fizzy frothing all around us as the jacuzzi jets start up. His arm tightens as I shift, startled by the swirling waves, then loosens again as I relax.

I've been in jacuzzi spas before, public ones in the gym or swimming pools, but never one that felt as fabulous as this one. The sensation is wonderful, a warm, soft, all-over massage. I let my legs drift upwards, floating, trusting Nathan to hold me, keep me afloat. I sip my juice then put the glass next to his, closing my eyes as I lay my head back on his shoulder. With his free hand he gently caresses my breast as we savour the sensuality of the music and the foaming, churning, gurgling spray tingling and swirling all around us. After a few minutes Nathan moves, shifting both of us more upright. His knees are between mine and he uses them to gently ease my legs apart, exposing my sensitive flesh to the jets shooting up from the bottom of the bath.

"Just wriggle around. Position yourself so it catches you just right, just where you like it most," he whispers in my ear. I do, and it feels fabulous, the warm disembodied pressure directly against my clitoris. I groan in ecstasy as he tightens his hold to keep me in position, holding me in place as the waves of delight flood over.

"Can you come like this or do you need more? Do you want me to help?" His whisper is low, husky. I can feel his erection hard and big under my bum and I wonder what 'help' he has in mind? Anything would be wonderful. I wriggle against him in answer and he chuckles softly, tipping me forward onto my knees. I reach for the opposite end of the bath with my hands, while Nathan spreads my knees as wide as the bath will allow. Which is pretty damn far.

He enters me quickly, slipping into me from behind whilst still making sure my clit continues to receive the full benefit of the jets shooting at me from below. He moves slowly, sliding in and out so tenderly I feel I could cry. This is gentle fucking with bells on! It's soothing, so, so comfortable, and so, so very slow. The tension and tug towards orgasm build little by little, softly, creeping up on me until I start to clench, shifting my body to increase the pressure, silently seeking more. But Nathan is ruthlessly unhurried and I have to wait, eventually tumbling sweetly, softly, into my climax. The familiar sparkle and internal fireworks shoot through me as I come, clenching around him, screwing my hips around as I instinctively bear down on him, begging him without words to increase the pressure on my sensitive inner walls. Responding at last he thrusts, sharp, hard, hitting that exact spot with unerring accuracy as I convulse, moaning, gasping my gratitude.

I feel the hot spurt inside me as he climaxes soon after I do, then he pulls me backwards to sit astride him. He is still buried deep inside me and apparently going nowhere, his finger now gently, lightly circling my clit. The effect is more one of calming than of arousal and I open my legs wide to appreciate it fully.

"Enjoying your bath, Miss Byrne," he murmurs.

I can only sigh, roll my shoulders in contentment. He gets the idea and lightly kisses the top of my head, continuing to caress me with his fingers. "Tell me how you feel, right now…" he whispers.

"I feel fine. This is so good."

"Your body feels fine, I can tell that. But what about your head?"

"My head?" I am at a loss, what is he after now?

"I can control how your body feels, pretty much. Pleasure, pain, I can deliver. On demand. Agreed?" Still bemused as to where this is going, but with a growing sense that it could be important, I try to gather my thoughts.

"Eva? Do you agree?"

He isn't letting up, so I answer, whispering, "Yes. Agreed."

"When we talked, in my office on Friday, you told me you wanted to explore the physical side of your sexuality. Did I understand that right?" At my silence he prompts, gently but insistent still. "Eva?"

"Yes, yes that's what I was trying to say. Not sure it came out quite like that, but yes."

"Okay. And you also said you wanted to understand, experience your emotions better. Relationships, being around other people, liking yourself and being liked, being loved... Did I get that right too?" This is much more personal. Much more intimate. But he's still spot on. Did I really say all that? Did I really let him see, hear all of that? Did I really hand him all that power to hurt me? And more to the point, starting to panic, can I get it back now?

"I, well, I'm not sure I meant. I mean, I do like myself. Obviously. Why wouldn't I?"

He's still gently stroking me, his cock still inside me, and I am struck by how incongruous this conversation seems to me. Not to him, though, apparently, as he continues, his voice steady, even, as though he might be addressing a business meeting or chatting across the breakfast table with Rosie.

"You tell me, love. What's not to like? Not to admire? You're clever, funny, talented, brave. You've got a body to die for, the most responsive little clit I've ever come across" — he pauses, flicks my clit lightly to emphasis his point — "if you'll pardon the pun, and you're the best lay I've ever had. And I've had a few, believe me, so I *am* an authority."

I can only gasp in reply — there's really no answer to that. He's not done yet, though. "I repeat, what's not to like? You're gorgeous, absolutely stunning. And brilliant too. The full package. I can't believe my luck that you turned up at my house that night. And that somehow I managed not to scare you away."

Does he mean me? He can't be talking about me. I am stunned. Absolutely speechless. No one, no one has ever spoken about me like that. No one ever thought of me like that. The best lay he's ever had? God! I should be affronted that it comes down to sex, but this is repressed, virginal little Eva Byrne we're talking about, flat-chested, nerdy little Eva Byrne, the boring swot with no tits, no friends and hair like a bunch of carrots. And somehow, incredibly, this gorgeous hunk of a man who knows more about sex and sensuality than anyone I've ever met, a one-man Karma Sutra, thinks I'm a good lay. Me! I could dance on the ceiling. Or failing that, I might just stroll across this ocean of a bathtub of his.

This can't be real. I have to ask. My voice cracking, I whisper, "Are you just saying all that? To make me feel better? Are you just being kind?"

"Well, I hope I'm being kind. I do try, most of the time. With you. And yeah, I do want you to feel good, Eva. But that doesn't mean I'm not telling you the truth, telling it like I see it. If you won't believe it from me, who would you like to hear it from? Is there someone else?" His voice is soft, gentle. No accusation here, no jealousy, just concern. For me.

It's too much. Compliments I can laugh off, admiration I can dismiss. But care and concern? Those just shoot straight through my carefully built defences and hit me direct in the heart. My face is wet, and I realise it's not only the bathwater. Intense emotion just undoes me. I can't handle it. Quite simply, I just never learnt how. Overwhelmed, with a gulp I turn in his arms and bury my face in his chest. I sob quietly as he holds me, strokes me, whispers sweet things in my hair.

"Beautiful, beautiful Eva. So sweet, so gorgeous, so sexy, so lovely... Talk to me, Eva. Cry if you need to. I'll wait, then we'll talk some more. Don't stop talking to me, sweetheart. Please. Promise me that, love."

My voice broken, halting, stumbling over the emotion surging through me, this strange, unfamiliar sensation that I don't know how to handle—yet—I manage to scrape together a near enough coherent reply. "I promise. I need you, Nathan. I need you to help me. Please don't stop helping me, caring about me."

"Caring comes easy, love. You've got that, always. And I'll help you if I can. For as long as you're here, as long as we're together, I'll be on your side. Okay? Believe me?"

"Yes, I believe you." *I love you. As long as I'm here. As long as I live.*

His voice is firmer now, the gentle lover receding. "Earlier, when I pulled you into the bath, you were...what? Being cocky? Defiant? Playing with me? Challenging me? Not very sub-like, Miss Byrne. I think you were feeling a little over-confident, yes? That it would be okay to push me a little?"

"Yes. I'm sorry."

"And I crushed it. Scared you. Put out the spark? Drowned it, I suppose would be more accurate?"

"Yes. Maybe. I didn't think of it like that."

"I never want to squash your spark, Eva. It's just a role. You do know that, don't you? Play-acting. We both play our parts, and it's fun. Well, I enjoy myself." He tips my chin up with his finger to look into my eyes, his questioning gaze light now, teasing.

"Me too." I smile, still a bit watery but managing to pull myself together.

"It's okay to be cocky. To say whatever you like to me. Always. I want you to know that. When we're in Dom-sub mode there are rules and I'll come on strong, intimidate you. Scare you, possibly. That's not real, though, never serious. But there's this other connection we have, these moments we have when you cry sometimes, usually when my cock's still inside you, like now."

Christ, how could I have forgotten that?

He nuzzles my neck as he continues, "When you share your secrets with me, when I listen, try to understand you. And that *is* real, that's not a game. And I want you to know you'll always be safe with me. Whether we're playing or not. Does that make sense?"

I nod. No words can help me to express the shell of safeness, of well-being he is building around me, within me. My gratitude, my appreciation, my sheer bloody wonder that he wants to be bothered. I put my arms around his neck and just squeeze him, tight. It's enough, he knows. And soon enough he eases me back around, careful not to let us disengage, and I am once more draped over him, my back against his chest as he feathers his clever, caring fingers across my body once more, my breasts, my tummy, stroking through the curls covering my pubic bone to slide between my legs.

For a few minutes the sensation is one of calm relaxation, before desire insistently kicks in again. It does for him too, as I feel his cock harden, growing and stiffening, stretching me from within. If anything, if it were possible, he feels even bigger this time. Despite my now far from virgin state I'm not sure I can manage this. I start to protest…

"It's okay love. You're okay. You're just very, very sensitive just now and it feels bigger. Enjoy. This is going to be one hell of a ride." Gently placing my hands back on the opposite rim he kneels up, and holding my hips firmly thrusts. Hard. I scream. He thrusts again, and again. And again. The pounding picks up a rhythm and I start to push back, strengthening the friction, pushing the pace. It's deep, powerful, relentless, made more raw by the pent-up passion now released, now surging though me after his emotional dam-busting exercise of a few minutes ago. I hang onto the bath and take it, take him, all of him. God, it's absolutely wonderful and my screams of pleasure are ringing around the room, drowning out Milos' efforts. My climax hits me moments before he collapses into his, and seconds later I am hanging onto the side of the bath, my cheek pressed against the warm teak, and I'm sucking in air as my senses slowly return.

"Okay, Miss Byrne. Work to do. Time to move on before we both end up like little wrinkled prunes." Sliding out of me at last, he pinches my bum, hard enough to make me squeal and jump up.

"What was that for?" I rub my abused bottom, glaring at him.

"For fun, love. Just for fun." He stands up, gloriously naked and dripping then strides over the side of the bath, using the step to leap down onto the floor. "You finish washing your hair while I get stuff ready out here. Don't be long, Miss Byrne." After leaning down to drop a kiss on my lips and wrap a towel around his hips he is gone.

I hurry with my hair, slapping a splodge of shampoo on and giving it all a quick rub, then rinsing with the small shower spray attached to the showy brass taps. I even spot some conditioner, 'specially formulated for frizzy, fly-away hair'. Nathan's hair is not even remotely frizzy so I can only assume he's got it just for me, the lovely man. I help myself, smoothing the creamy, calming lotion through the length of my hair, finger combing it into some sort of order before setting to again with the shower spray.

At last I'm done, I think, so I clamber out. I poke around the side of the bath and find the switch to still the foaming water, then I press the lever to let out the plug. With a soft little gurgle the huge bath starts to empty. I help myself to a large fluffy towel and wrap myself in it, then grab another smaller one for my hair. I twist my hair in it turban-style, and check out my reflection in the full-length mirrors opposite me. My face is pink from the steam and our exertions in the bath — the flush accentuated perhaps by the contrast with the creamy fluffiness of the towels.

Nervous about the coming prospect, I find myself playing for time. I drift over to the double sink unit and help myself to one of the toothbrushes there, quickly brushing my teeth. I check them with a growly smile in the mirror, wondering if he'll mind me nicking his toothbrush when I could have easily gone to fetch mine from the en suite in the bedroom.

Then I give my hair a blow-dry with the wired in hairdryer clipped into its holster next to the mirror, the sort of thing you sometimes find in hotels. Leaving the slightly damp copper and amber tendrils loose around my shoulders I find a long dark navy towelling robe—very masculine—hanging next to the shower cubicle and decide to borrow it. It seems more secure, more decent, than my towel so I slip my arms through it and tie the belt. Tight.

At last, stalling over, I take a deep breath, then another, and turn to leave.

I expect Nathan to be waiting in the bedroom, but instead he is in the dining area. And clearly this is where he intends to perform the next instalment of my adventure. Wearing just his jeans now, zipped but unbuttoned, he has laid a couple of towels over the dining table, and piled cushions in the middle. An angle poise lamp is positioned at one end, throwing a spotlight down the length of the table. He has pulled a small trolley alongside, similar to the sort of thing Damien had for his rollers and foils when he transformed my crowning glory a couple of days ago. But Nathan has collected strips of cloth by the look of it, a handful of flat wooden lolly sticks, a pair of scissors, tweezers, a bottle of baby lotion, and has a bowl of something in his hand, which he is stirring slowly. He looks up as I come in, then drops his gaze back to his bowl.

"You took your time. Still, your problem. The softer your skin is for this the better so it's best to do it immediately after a bath. Not half an hour later. And those painkillers won't last forever so let's get on, now you're finally here. Would you mind climbing onto the table, Miss Byrne? On your back please."

"I didn't realise. You should have told me." One sardonic eyebrow quirks as he looks at me across the table, shrugging. "And anyway, what's wrong with the bedroom? I could stretch out on the bed, more comfortable..." I ask, still hedging for time, though by now I should know that's quite pointless.

"You're not going to be comfortable wherever we do it. And it's too messy. And the light's better in here. Don't want to miss any of your important little places, Miss Byrne. And the microwave's handy — for heating the wax," he explains helpfully.

Out of excuses I shrug, and slide onto the table, bum first then swing my legs up. I position myself carefully on my back, as instructed, on the towels. I arrange the cushions under my head and make myself comfortable. *I wish.*

Nathan glances at me and puts the bowl on the trolley, striding off into the bedroom. He comes back moments later with two pillows. "Sorry, I forgot about the head end. These are for under your bum. Lift up."

I oblige, thrusting my hips upwards and he pushes both bulky pillows under me, raising my bottom a good foot off the table top.

"You can keep the bathrobe on if you like." I nod, hugging it closer across my breasts. "Just hitch up the bottom. Push it up above your waist, and lie back."

I do as I'm told, lifting the robe to expose my body, naked from the waist down. I shouldn't be self-conscious by now but I am, and I move to push a corner back, just enough to cover my groin. He smiles, shakes his head, and gets on with the matter in hand.

"Right up above your waist, Miss Byrne, please."

Resigned, I do as he asks and close my eyes, waiting.

"I'm going to remove all the hair this first time. Miss Byrne. Maybe later, when it grows back, we'll leave this bit, just keep it short perhaps, because it is a truly lovely shade of red." He is casually combing his fingers through the golden ginger curls covering my pubic bone. "Open your legs."

I do, and he slips his hand between, gently tugging the wispy strands of hair around my vagina. "This all goes. And stays gone." Lifting my knee with one hand he reaches lower, his fingers circling my now exposed anus and reaching between the cheeks of my bum. I close my eyes, mortified, not least as I didn't even realise I had hair there. I do. I definitely do. I feel the light tug as he draws it between his fingers. "This too, definitely."

I feel desperately vulnerable, exposed, lying on the table, my legs spread wide open while he examines me critically, his fingers cool and businesslike. I instinctively tense when he picks up a small pair of scissors.

"Keep still, Miss Byrne. We don't want any accidents." He repositions the lamp at the opposite end of the table to shine directly between my legs. He turns so his back is to me as he leans over to pay close attention to my groin, and he starts to snip at the hair.

I lie there, silent, aware of every touch, every slight pull as he eases the hair taut then clips it, dropping the discarded bits into a small pile beside me. He quickly trims the hair at the front then, lifting my right leg and bending it at the knee he shoves it outwards. My left leg is lying straight. He leans over a little more, adjusts the lamp, and continues to clip the hair. I feel his fingers parting the lips of my vagina to reach every strand, gently nudging around my clitoris. He pushes my bent leg down and repeats the action with the left one opening the other side of my most private place for his detailed scrutiny and intimate examination.

With his finger he again eases my vagina open, dispassionately stroking my labia as he clips and tidies, preparing me for the ultimate humiliation.

I am beyond mortified. I close my eyes, will myself to lie still, to take it, and I just wish it was over.

It seems to take ages, but in reality must have only been a couple of minutes before he straightens, and glances back at me. "You okay, Miss Byrne? Quite comfortable?"

"No. I hate this. Please, just hurry up. Get it over with."

"Happy to oblige, as ever, Miss Byrne. Lift your leg, bend it at the knee and let it drop to the side, nice and wide for me, please." And I do as I am told, dutifully lifting and bending my right leg to expose my groin.

Facing me this time, he takes the bowl from the trolley. Using one of the wooden spatulas, he scoops out a blob of wax, smoothing it quickly along one side of my vulva. It feels very warm, hot, just short of painful. He then takes a strip of fabric and presses it into the hot wax, and I stiffen, waiting for the pain as he tears it off. I am not to be disappointed.

"Christ!" I scream as, with a sharp ripping sound, the fabric, wax and hairs are torn viciously from my body. My sensitive skin is smarting, burning. Only his right arm, flung across my stomach and holding me firmly in place stops me from leaping from the table. Keeping me pinned in place with his arm he uses his right hand to pull the skin and delicate folds around my vagina taut and his left hand to mercilessly repeat the action. He works down and around my most sensitive skin, opening the delicate lips and sharply, ruthlessly, painfully removing all and every stray hair.

My eyes are watering, the pain sharp and cruel, and I cry out with every tearing pull. Undeterred, ignoring my struggles, he continues, occasionally glancing up at me, warning me to keep still if I can. I can't, so he holds me down, offering to tie my hands behind my back if that might help…

Realising I'm beaten I concentrate on getting through it, and actually, the pain does seem to lessen as he continues. Either he's getting more skilled or I'm just becoming numbed by the relentless, repeated assaults. Or maybe those bloody painkillers are doing their job at last. He straightens, lowers my bent knee back to the table and, gesturing, indicates that I should open the other side for him. Biting my lip, I do as I'm told. He bends once more to his task, and I scream again as a new wave of pain hits me.

Carefully, he repeats the treatment. The sound is savage, almost as dreadful as the pain. Almost. I can only guess at how this might have felt without the paracetamol earlier. I grit my teeth, close my eyes and concentrate on trying to keep still.

Once the lips of my vagina are suitably hairless, to his apparent satisfaction, he moves forward to concentrate on the delicate folds shielding my clitoris. Again he opens them, spreading the sensitive lips wide to cover them in the wax. "Please, not there," I beg, suddenly terrified at the prospect of what might be coming next, and writhing under his hands as I anticipate the agony of having the wax torn from my clitoris itself.

"No, sweetheart, not there," he murmurs gently, and I relax again. Slightly.

The pain is sharp, but bearable now, and I breathe slowly, riding it as he finishes and at last my groin area is smooth and hairless. He runs his fingers over my sensitive, tender, inflamed flesh, through the folds, around the entrance to my vagina, around my clitoris, the light from his lamp exposing every corner as he searches for any stray hairs. He finds one, close to my vagina on the left side and swiftly removes it with tweezers.

"This stuff is tougher, and tends to be a bit more painful. I'll be really quick, though." He is spreading wax over the trimmed hair at the apex of my thighs, and quickly presses on the fabric. I hold my breath as the wax cools and sticks, and let it out in an agonised scream as he tears the first strip away. The fabric is full of hairs, ripped out at the roots. He repeats the action twice more, still holding me firmly in place as, grimly determined, he finishes his task. As quickly as he began, it seems he is finished, running the backs of his fingers over my newly smooth body.

"So far so good. Sit up, Miss Byrne, see what you think of your new look?"

"Have you done?" I struggle up onto my elbows, looking down to survey the damage. Oddly, much to my surprise, I find I like it. I am smooth, soft and sleek. Nathan squirts a blob of baby lotion onto his fingers and gently smears it over my stinging flesh, cooling, soothing and comforting. I wince, but find myself willingly opening my legs to let him reach all of me.

I smile, my face split into a beaming grin as I examine myself critically. I look...lovely. I hadn't ever given a thought to my pubic hair before, it was just— there, sort of red and springy like the rest of my thatch. Now it isn't and I like my new look. Clean, sexy and begging to be touched.

"Hey, that looks fantastic. I should have done this ages ago..." I grin at him cheekily as he shakes his head wryly.

"No beauty salon would have put up with all the fuss you made, love. All that screaming would be bad for business."

A thought occurs suddenly, an uncomfortable, disturbing thought. "I look like a little girl. A child…"

He continues to massage the cool lotion into my delicate skin, easing his fingers gently between the folds and the lips of my vagina. He glances up at me, an amused smile across his handsome face.

"Well, you're certainly female, Miss Byrne, and I grant you are a little on the small side, but a little girl? Never. Oh no. You are most definitely a woman, and a seriously lovely woman at that. Hot. Responsive." He slides two fingers inside me, then swiftly out again to caress my clitoris, to emphasis his point, and I arch in response.

"Okay, turn over. Just the last little bit of hair to deal with."

"What, I thought you'd finished. What now?" I glare at him in frustration.

"We're nearly done. Turn over, Eva. Now, please." That stern Dom voice again.

I know better than to argue with him in Dom mode and roll onto my stomach, eying him warily over my shoulder. Deftly he pushes both my knees up so I find myself in a squat, my face resting on the cushions and my bum in the air. Talk about exposed and vulnerable… And with him in this mood. Christ!

However, his hands are gentle as he eases my buttocks apart to examine the skin around my anus.

I shudder, wishing I was anywhere else but here right now. Almost.

"What are you doing, Nathan? God, this is awful. Talk about humiliating. If you even think about picking up a cane I'm out of here." He needs telling.

He just chuckles. "No cane. For now, anyway. But later, definitely." He picks up the bowl of wax again, and I brace myself for what's coming. "Almost done. Just hold still, love." The endearment, so rare from Nathan the Dom, calms me. I let him smooth the hot wax onto my delicate skin, stiffening as he presses the fabric strips in and stands back, waiting for it to harden. Holding my buttocks apart, he stretches my skin tight with one hand and rips the first strip away. I gasp, but manage not to scream and hold myself still for him to repeat the process. Three more times I have to bite back my screams, clutching at the cushions, my knuckles white.

At last he puts the wax bowl back onto the trolley, and now I feel his fingers gently probing my inflamed genitals. He angles the light, looking for any remaining hairs that may have escaped his attention, finding just a couple, which he deals with quickly with his tweezers. Then I feel something cool, blissfully, wonderfully cool, and his palm brushing over me as he smears the soothing lotion all over my exposed, throbbing, sorely abused anal area. "Just some more baby lotion, to get rid of any wax that's still there and to take the sting out. I'm guessing you like this bit, Miss Byrne. You've stopped screaming. At last. Now, don't move."

His hands drop away and I moan in frustration.

"Lift your bum up a little more, please, Miss Byrne, and open your legs as wide as you can."

Quivering, I do as I am told. The last thing I expect is to hear the quiet, whirring hum of a camera.

"Hey, what the...? I never said you could photograph me!" I whirl round, ready to do battle for the camera, lurid visions of my genitals being plastered all over YouTube clamouring through my mind.

"Whoah, Eva," he laughs, holding the mobile phone way up out of my reach as I hop up and down, still kneeling on the table and trying to grab it from him. "Calm down. You can delete the pictures soon. We'll keep them just for now, though. I'll show you why." And with that he shoves the phone back in the pocket of his jeans and grabs me around the waist, hauling me up into his arms, still a bundle of near-naked, spitting fury. He turns and makes for the bedroom, grabbing the bottle of baby lotion.

"Here, you take this—" And I find it shoved into my hands.

Still minded to brain him with the bloody baby lotion I am dumped unceremoniously on the brown leather settee in his bedroom, the scene of my unfortunate mishap of yesterday morning. I am struck by how far I've come since then. Maybe. I hope...

"Take the robe off now, kneel on the seat and lean over the back," he says curtly. "And spread your legs. Wide."

"Not bloody likely! For you to take more porno shots?" I sit mutinously, enveloped in the navy blue robe, my knees hugged against my chest, glowering at him.

He takes the phone from his pocket and hands it to me.

"There, Miss Byrne. You've got the phone and I promise no more pictures without warning you first. So, drop the robe. I want you naked for this. And assume the position." At my continuing hesitation his eyes narrow, glinting coldly. "Don't make me wait, Eva."

"Are you going to tie me up again? And how come you're never bloody naked for this stuff?" My voice is shaky. I start to shiver, remembering the last time I was here. And he's so angry now, cruel and intimidating as he stands in front of me, his eyes hard, his voice cold.

"No, I'm not going to tie you up. Well, not yet anyway. Unless I need to, to make you do as you're told. And I explained before why I like you naked. Don't make this difficult, Eva. You won't like the consequences."

He gestures with his hand that I need to bend over and present my backside, no doubt for a seriously hard spanking to teach me something about the consequences of belligerence. There's no other realistic alternative for me now, so, shaking, I do as I'm told. At last.

Nathan takes the baby lotion from me as I turn to face the back of the settee, the bottle still clutched in one hand, the phone in the other. "Thanks. We haven't finished with this yet. I expect you'd appreciate some more, would you? To take the sting away. Open your legs then, Miss Byrne."

I do, but not enough it would seem.

"Wider, please, and lean farther over to lift your bum up. Show me what you've got there."

Clutching the phone in my hand I lean forward, lifting up my bum, and I wait. And wait. Tense, expecting the sharp slap of his palm or maybe worse to land on my perfectly positioned bottom at any moment. He moves to stand behind me and I flinch. But Nathan is in no hurry—he knows the effect this agony of waiting is having on me and is milking it. I know he's looking at me, looking at my genitals presented there for him in all their naked glory. The humiliation, the fear, the tension are nearly overwhelming as the seconds tick by, becoming minutes.

I scream in shock as he feathers one gentle finger lightly along my clit, jerking involuntarily.

"Did I hurt you?" His voice is soft, quiet, barely a whisper.

"No. It was just... I just..." I never used to stammer like this, and I clench my fist around his phone as I force myself to remain still, in this exposed position, waiting for the next touch.

The next touch comes, and it is cool, moist, as he spreads a liberal squirt of baby lotion around my clitoris. And then more of the soothing lotion, quickly, efficiently smoothing it all over my exposed sex and drawing upwards towards my anus. He gently works it into every fold, every secret place—not that I have any secrets left it seems to me. Except one, and he's on it now. He pulls my buttocks apart and he squirts the lotion directly onto my anus. It feels cool, and so wickedly good.

I sigh, pushing any embarrassment aside to savour the intimate caresses as he continues to probe and stroke my over-sensitised genitals, paying more attention than perhaps strictly necessary to my tight little virgin arse. I gasp as he slowly eases his little finger through the sphincter, turning it slowly to smear the cooling lotion inside as well as around the outer rim.

"So sweet, Eva, so sweet. Your gorgeous arse is crying out for some serious attention."

Maybe. And it's getting it too. I feel his finger probing again, pressing into that last secret place, that forbidden, private place. At first just the tip, then more as his finger gently, slowly, eases inside. Right inside, the whole length. He leaves it there for a few moments, gently circling to widen, open my tight entrance, sliding back out only to slip back in, penetrating me fully again. I groan, but not with pain. Not yet pleasure either. The sensation is…familiar, but oh so strange.

"Are you okay?" He leans over me to whisper the question into my ear.

I murmur back, "Yes. I'm okay. It feels so weird, though."

"You're doing really well, angel. Relax. You can do this. You can let me do this." He withdraws his finger and I feel something cool and wet—baby lotion no doubt, dribbling into my now looser arse, through the entrance and down into my back passage. Then his finger again, but not the little one this time. This time it's bigger, longer, and it pushes harder, more insistently as my body suddenly surrenders. I give up any hope of keeping him out and allow my muscles to relax, accepting this invasion. He strokes the cheeks of my bottom gently as he takes full advantage of my surrender, working another finger into my arse alongside the first. It feels full, stretched tight, wickedly tight. I am gasping now, moaning as the pleasure kicks in. He works his fingers in and out a few more times, a few deep strokes to make sure I really am conquered before he reaches his other hand down between my legs to stroke my clit.

The effect is instantaneous—I go off like a rocket. This orgasm is powerful, punching through me, brutal and exquisite, exploding out through my fingers and toes as I rock back against his hand, begging for more, for harder, for faster. His fingers on my clit and inside me are slick and skilful, and the moment is drawn out, dragged to the extreme as I convulse helplessly. I may have screamed. Probably. I am certainly gasping for air as the pulsing eventually subsides and I return to reality. The reality of his fingers still deep in my butt and my hips gyrating, asking wordlessly for more.

"Stay there, Eva. Don't move." He gently withdraws his fingers and I moan, settling my face over my folded arms along the back of the settee to wait. He gently prises the phone from my grip, and I release it without argument, willing to let him have anything he wants at that moment.

"One more quick picture, love, okay?"

"Mmmm. What?" I mutter, still dazed from my orgasm, then I hear the tell-tale whirr of the camera again. I start to push myself up, but he is quicker. Sweeping me into his arms he carries me effortlessly to the bed and lays me on my back, lying beside me. Before I can protest about more pictures he is kissing me, deeply, sensuously, his tongue deep in my mouth, tangling with mine. Stopping only long enough to pull the phone from his pocket and toss it onto the pillow, he unzips his jeans and kicks them off. Then he is above me, his knees between mine, easing my legs apart. I take no persuading, and he slips inside me, his huge erection stretching me deliciously, filling me.

"God you're beautiful, Eva. You feel so good. So tight." He eases back, and into me once more, to the hilt, his cock nudging my cervix. I moan, arch, stretching under him, my arms outstretched above my head. This is bliss. Sheer, absolute, bloody bliss. My hips are gyrating as I thrust back, trying to increase the pressure, find more friction, more sensation.

"Yes, angel, yes. Take me, take all of me. God I adore you, so sweet, so fucking sweet..." He slips his hands under my bottom to lift me, holding me to him and angling my hips so he can hit *that* spot, with every long, hard stroke.

I come quickly with a fractured cry, my whole body loose, melting around him. He stills, his face tight with intense concentration as he fights for control while I convulse and writhe under him. When I am still again he starts to move, slowly, gently, his hand slipping between us to stroke my clitoris until once more I am thrashing with passion, desperately reaching for yet another climax. It dances just out of reach, then I have it, and I am once more circling out of control, sparks shooting through every part of me as I squeeze around him. With a low growl he slams into me hard as his own climax takes over. He thrusts again, and again, and I jolt under the power and fury of it, delighted almost as much at his pleasure as I am at my own.

At last it is over. We are still, quiet, the only sound our ragged breathing as we lie motionless, a mass of twisted limbs and tangled sheets. He makes no move to shift his weight from me, and I make no move to remind him. We are simply fine, together.

Eventually Nathan rolls over on to his back and, piling pillows behind him, he props himself up against the headboard. He pulls me up alongside, his left arm slung around my shoulders. In his right hand he has the phone, which he clicks on. With a few strokes on the screen he has my porno pictures up, in glorious Technicolor. He holds the phone for me to see, and I cringe.

"Please, delete them. I don't want you having pictures of me. Please." I look up at him, pleading. How could I have let him take those shots? How could he have done it to me?

"You can delete them yourself, Eva. In a minute. First, though, do you see a difference between the two shots?" He toggles between them. I don't want to look but he nudges me, insisting I pay attention.

"Do you see a difference, Eva?"

I take the phone and look carefully. There is a difference. Subtle, but definitely not the same. Are both pictures of me?

"Yes, Eva, they are both you."

Uh-oh, more thinking aloud, getting to be a dodgy habit.

Flicking to one photo he holds the phone up in front of me. "This is the first picture I took, right after I finished waxing you. This is your not-a-chuckly-teddy look. This is you not enjoying yourself. Definitely not aroused. You hated the waxing, didn't you?" At my silence he prompts. "Eva, didn't you? It's a good thing my nearest neighbours are three floors down or someone might have called the police, the din you made."

I grimace, remembering, and he kisses the top of my head.

Using his thumb to scroll through he brings up the other picture. "This one, on the other hand, this is your fuck-me-please, I'm-gagging-for-it look. This was what you looked like after I made you come with my fingers in your arse, before I fucked you just now. In this picture you are definitely aroused. Can you see what's different, Eva?"

Embarrassed I shake my head. There's something, definitely, but I'm not sure specifically what. I look again at the second shot, a perfect view of my own genitals, pretty and naked and very, very exposed. Wow.

"Mmm, wow indeed." He agrees. Did I say that out loud? Apparently so. I really must try to watch that. "Pretty bloody amazing. Beautiful, in fact. Ready for a biology lesson, Miss Byrne?"

"What do you mean? I know what all the bits are." I am somewhat indignant. "A level biology says I know my way around the female genitalia."

"Only A level? You disappoint me, Eva. Still, it's a start. We can work with that."

"Grade A!" I interrupt, indignant.

"Naturally, Miss Byrne. May I continue?"

I nod somewhat sullenly it has to be said.

"Thank you. Now allow me to take you on a guided tour round your own genitalia, your aroused genitalia, that is. First, compare the colour—you're much pinker, darker in the second picture. And look at your clitoris." He toggles between the two and I see that in the second picture my clit is much bigger, swollen. So are the lips of my vagina. It's really very obvious now he's pointed it out.

"Do you see how your clit has swollen? That's one way I know for sure when you're enjoying whatever I'm doing to you. Through the pain, under the pain. You might ask me to stop, but if your clit's swollen and pink, if your nipples are hard like little red pebbles and if the lips at the entrance to your vagina are swollen and pink too that tells me that whatever your mouth might be saying, your body's fucking loving it. You've seen enough now, Eva. Delete the pictures if you want." He hands me the phone, and leans over me, his gaze gentle, serious, a soft smile on his lips. Lifting my knees with his hand he gently pushes them apart, the backs of his fingers lightly stroking between my legs. His gaze leaves my face to fix on a point beyond the end of the bed. I follow it, and see myself reflected in the mirror on the wardrobe door, my newly hairless genitals in all their glory. Instinctively I make to close my legs, but he pushes them open again. Bloody hell, am I to have no secrets?

"There's pleasure/pain Eva, and that's what I show you. And then there's just pain. The nasty sort. Your body knows the difference. Your head still has to learn. But you're a fast learner, so we'll work on it."

"Today? Will we be working on it today?"

"Not today. It's still too soon. You need to get over yesterday. And now, I think you need to get some sleep, sweetheart."

I hadn't realised I was yawning, but he's right. I am bone weary, again. He pulls me close and I snuggle into his chest, my arm slung across him. "Tomorrow then..." I murmur as he pulls the duvet around us.

"Mmm, we'll see." The quiet whisper brushes my ear as he bends to kiss my hair, and I feel safe again.

Chapter Four

When I awaken I am alone, tucked up warm and cosy in Nathan's bed. I glance across at the clock. Two twenty. I have been asleep for a couple of hours. I stretch, allowing my fingers to drift downwards to explore my new, hair-free body. I slide my fingers over the mound where my flame-coloured thatch used to be, and I definitely like this feel better. Smooth, sort of peachy. It really is rather nice. I probe further, spreading my legs now to reach between them. The sensation is really very pleasant, much more enjoyable than my previous fumbles in this department, but not nearly so exquisite as when Nathan touches me. But I'm loving the smooth silkiness of my skin, the wetness instantly starting to gather and pool as I stroke my clit. I can feel the sensitive little nub swelling under my hands, and I'm just wondering about looking around for the mirror to aid my voyage of discovery when I become aware of sounds from elsewhere in the apartment. I lie still for a few seconds, listening.

I can hear the low hum of the television out in the lounge area and suddenly want to be out there with Nathan. Not in here, alone. I slip out of bed and retrieve my — well, Nathan's — dark navy bathrobe from behind the leather sofa. Tying the belt I pad barefoot into the lounge.

Nathan is lying on the settee. At first he doesn't realise I am there, his attention riveted on the television where Team GB is gearing up for great things in the Olympic velodrome. I approach soundlessly, planting a kiss on the top of his head from behind.

His reflexes are good, I'll grant him that as he shoots out his arm, grabs me and tumbles me forward over the back of the settee. I land in his lap, my bathrobe unceremoniously tangled around my shoulders leaving my bum exposed. Never one to miss an opportunity Nathan holds me, wriggling, across his knee and lands several hard slaps on my rump. I squeal, laughing as he lets me go and I scramble up to take his gorgeous face between my palms and kiss him again, deeply. He is badly in need of a shave and the stubble is scratchy, sexy. I lift my head to look into his twinkling, dark chocolate eyes, and he winks at me.

"Nice nap, Miss Byrne?"

"Mmm, lovely. What now? What are we doing today?"

"Chilling. Watching the Olympics. Care to join me?" He shifts me around so I am lying alongside him on the settee, our legs intertwined.

"Sounds great. Mind if I get a cup of tea and a snack first, though? I'm starving."

"Is that a hint I'm not looking after you properly, Miss Byrne? Stay there." He pushes easily to his feet and heads over to the kitchen.

"I didn't mean... I didn't want to disturb you. I can get my own tea."

"If you're feeling energetic get the guitar and show me how well you can play it. I fancy another of your private little concerts, Miss Byrne. Then I might have to jump your bones again, sadly. Can't be helped. You're very, very sexy when you play, do you know that?" He tosses the careless compliments back over his shoulder as he grabs a couple of mugs from a cupboard and fills the kettle.

Always in my element when playing music, whatever the instrument, I'm happy to comply. I look around for the guitar and spot it still propped against the kitchen worktop where I left it. I scramble off the settee and fetch it. Coming back, I perch on the edge of the settee, cradling the instrument across my knees, strumming lightly and listening to the tone. Instinctively I turn the tuning keys ever so slightly, quite unnecessarily as I tuned it only a couple of hours or so ago. Nathan comes back, placing a tray on the coffee table in front of me, carrying two steaming mugs of tea and a plate of chocolate Bourbon biscuits.

"My favourites." He smiles, nibbling on one as he sits on the settee opposite me, leaning back to enjoy my performance.

"Any requests?" I ask, glancing across at him, remembering that first time I played for him, in the kitchen at Black Combe. His answer is the same now as it had been then. "No. You choose."

I nod, and strum a few experimental chords before picking up the old Ralph McTell classic, *Streets of London*. Never much of a singer I hum along, bending over the instrument, rocking slightly and glancing up from time to time to find his attention unwavering, fixed on me. When I finish I sit back, smiling. I'm not an especially accomplished guitarist, not by my normal standards, but I can get by well enough. And I love music, I just love playing, whatever the instrument.

Nathan clearly appreciates my efforts. "As ever, Miss Byrne, you impress me. I get hard just looking at you with an instrument in your hands. Particularly mine." He winks. "Maybe you could give me guitar lessons. And did I mention how very sexy you are when you're performing for me? That first time, when you played *Bolero,* it was all I could do not to fuck you senseless there and then. Interesting choice of music that night, I must say. Very sensual, provocative. I rather thought you might be gagging for it. I was, definitely. But with Rosie and Grace there, I thought best not..."

Entering into the spirit I return the banter. "Pity. I can see your problem, though. And you've so made up for it since." I grin at him cheekily, loving the suggestive tit-for-tat, another first for me. Then, my curiosity and innate seriousness getting the better of me, I ask the question uppermost in my mind at this moment. "How come you've got a guitar, but you don't play? And a piano?"

I am puzzled. I just can't see why anyone would own two such beautiful instruments and never use them. The beautiful piano back at Black Combe graces the large dining room but had stood there untouched, for years I gather, before I got my hands on it.

"The guitar was a present from my brother. He thought I needed a hobby. And I bought the piano because I like it. It's a nice thing." He reaches for another Bourbon.

"Hmph, your brother obviously doesn't know you very well. If he knew where your interests really lay he'd have bought you whips and a set of handcuffs. Don't you two get on?" The words slip out before I realise what I'm saying, and I look up tentatively.

To my relief Nathan is still smiling, leaning forward to pick up his mug. He takes a sip. "Me and my brother get on just fine, Miss Byrne, and I suspect Daniel has an idea regarding my 'interests' as you put it. I rather suspect he shares them—sort of a family failing you might say. But I already have lots of whips and handcuffs, as you well know. And now I have a guitar too. Which would you prefer to play with this afternoon?"

"Does he know about your whips and chains? Daniel?"

"I'm sure he does. And, Miss Byrne, it's handcuffs, not chains. Although I prefer a nice piece of rope personally. You seem very determined to discuss my other toys. Should I fetch a pair of handcuffs for you, demonstrate how they work? Or would you rather play me another tune?"

In response I grip the guitar neck and bend over it again. Feeling a little of the same challenge I felt that first night at Black Combe I'm determined to use this opportunity to show off my skills, my talents. And quite consciously to manipulate the situation, if only to prove to myself I can. I want to play something sensual, sexy, arousing, and after a moment or two's thought I settle for an acoustic version of *Something*, by George Harrison.

I have Nathan's complete attention, as before. He leans back in the settee, his eyes never leaving me.

Even though I never look up from the instrument I can feel his dark, brooding gaze on my bent head as I stretch my fingers across the neck of the guitar to form the chords, strumming softly. Eventually the soft melody ends and the last strains die away. Neither of us makes a move. Not wanting to discuss whips and handcuffs again, at least not for a while, I decide to try something a little more ambitious. This is a lovely instrument, responsive. I've become attuned to it, this might work.

I lean over the guitar again and start another piece, this time a classical melody but one made famous as a film soundtrack, as so many are. This piece is written for classical guitar and sounds superb when played unplugged. Under my fingers the sensuous, romantic, melody of *Cavatina* by Stanley Myers floats into the room, haunting, atmospheric. And it seems to fit the mood today quite well.

Nathan is listening idly, obviously content to let me strum away, but he comes to attention as I start this last piece, as he recognises it. His eyes are on me, I can feel them, intense, burning, even though I never take mine off the neck of the guitar where I'm carefully working the steel strings with my fingers. The fingering is complicated, and I'm playing pretty much by ear — I need to concentrate. The lovely, haunting melody fills the room, soars around us, caresses us. The passion and tragedy within the piece is drawn out by the nakedness of the delivery, just as it was intended. No frills, no fancy electronic treatment. Just me, a guitar and a beautiful piece of music.

"I recognise that, I've heard it before somewhere." Nathan's words are murmured softly as the last strains die away. I glance up, meet his eyes, which are dark, almost black. This time we're alone, and I know what comes next.

"That was superb, again, Eva. What was it?" The question is voiced softly, Nathan leaning forward to gaze at me.

"*Cavatina*, by Stanley Myers." His blank look tells me he needs more. "It was the theme tune to *The Deer Hunter*."

"Ah, yes. I remember now. A lovely piece, and played so beautifully. And deliberately? I think you know the effect it had on me, and what happens next?" I do, but still he makes no move. And then, "Is that how you think of me, Eva? As a hunter? A predator? Have I caught you?" The soft voice is gentle, caressing, the question a serious one.

Appreciating the significance of the moment I don't answer immediately, considering his words. Maybe my choice was not so random after all. I suspect that nothing ever is in my world.

At last, I answer, "I happened across your path, and you caught me. Perhaps. But it was me who was hunting. And I found."

Smiling softly he reaches over to take the guitar and places it back in its case. "You certainly did, thank God. And so did I." He hesitates, watching me, then continues, his voice low and seductive, "You know I need to fuck you now, don't you? I think that was the idea, yes?"

"Yes," I whisper, marvelling at my own new-found power to affect events.

"Here?"

It seems I have a choice of location too. Is there no end to my powers? I nod. "Here's good," I whisper, looking across the coffee table at him. He holds my gaze, his chocolate eyes sexy and sensual, his arousal obvious.

"Any particular preferences, Little Eva? What would you like to do?"

I think for a moment, then smile, remembering. "That thing you did last night, when you were inside me and you stroked me, stroked my clit, until I came. And came. And came. Can you do that again? Please?"

"It will be my absolute pleasure, Miss Byrne."

And it was mine too. Absolutely.

* * * *

Later, our long cold teacups replenished, Nathan sits down next to me on the settee. He picks up my mug and places it in my hands. "Here, drink your tea before it goes cold again, you insatiable little beast. I made Earl Grey for you. Fancy a Bourbon?"

I sip and nibble in silence, his arm lightly slung over my shoulders while Nathan's attention drifts back to the Olympics. The cycling has long since given way to high diving, and find myself watching enviously as the lean, athletic bodies angle gracefully through the air to land with hardly a ripple.

I murmur absently, "I wish I could swim."

"What's this, Miss Byrne, something you can't actually do? Maybe there's hope for my battered ego yet."

"I never learnt. It looks like fun, though. And you never know when it might be useful. When someone might toss you into a huge bath and try to drown you, for example." I peep up at him, and he tightens his arm around me.

"Like I said, if I decide to drown you, you'll know. I'll swap you swimming lessons for guitar lessons, though. Deal?"

"What? You'll teach me to swim? Why?" I turn around, staring at him, amazed.

"Why not? Like you said, might be fun. And useful. You might fall off a boat…"

"I tend to avoid boats. Are you a swimmer? Is that how you keep your body so, well, so perfect?"

"I scuba dive. And surf a bit. So yes, I do need to swim. But I only do that stuff in warm water so not that often. Since you ask, my main sport is karate. I'm at the dojo two or three times a week. When I can manage it."

I'm surprised. I might have seen him as a weekend cricketer, or maybe playing rugby. Definitely working out at some expensive gym. But martial arts? There's a turn-up. "Are you any good?"

"Black belt, fourth Dan. So yes, I'm pretty good." He finishes his tea and puts the mug down, turning to me. "More than a match for you, Miss Byrne, but I think I've already proved that. The kick boxing is on soon. I do a bit of that too, but I'm not especially good. Still, I was going to watch it, might pick up some tips." He nods in the direction of the Olympic coverage on the television, settling into the settee next to me. "Care to join me?"

"Mmm, sounds good." I snuggle in, tucking my feet under me.

We enjoy a few minutes of companionable silence as the divers do their thing. I'm not especially interested in sport, but who can't be caught up in the patriotism of Olympic fever. London 2012. Inspire a generation. Certainly, something's inspired me recently.

Long minutes pass as we watch the athletes' endeavours in admiring silence. Then, "Don't you wish you were there?"

"What? Where?"

"There. London. You could be seeing all this live if you'd been at home this summer."

"London's not my home. My mother lives there, not me."

"Oh. I thought you said you drove up from London. That night. In the rain."

"Yes, from my mother's flat."

"I see. Where do you live then? Where's home?"

This is it. I've been dreading this conversation, but it was always going to happen. Might as well tell it like it is. Well, some of it. "I lived in Oxford until a few weeks ago, at St Hilda's College. But I left. Suddenly. I can't go back."

I sense his sudden alertness, his attention fixed on me. His tone is harder, more exacting now. "Can't? Why can't?"

"I just can't, that's all. Just leave it, it's not important."

Not the response he was expecting, and not what he's prepared to accept. His body stiffens, he sits up straight. His voice has hardened — the steel is back with a vengeance. Clearly my reluctance to share on this occasion is not going to wash, but I'm not exactly certain why it matters this time. Obviously it does, though and he's not letting me off the hook.

"Were you sacked from your job? The truth, Eva. What happened?"

Suddenly, from almost nowhere, it's back. That overwhelming sense of panic, that desperation to escape. That black cloud that I managed, eventually, to crawl out of so many weeks ago is surrounding me once more, smothering me. Choking me. All the suppressed emotion, the thinly veiled terror that has been hovering just below the surface re-emerges with a vengeance. I leap to my feet, start for the bedroom. Anything, anywhere, just as long as it's away from Nathan. Nathan and his prying questions, his suspicious hostility. Why couldn't he just let it be?

He snags my wrist as I pass him and he drags me back onto the settee, close to him, his hand circling my wrist to keep me there. His grip is firm, almost painful, his eyes glittering in sudden anger.

"Answer me, damn it. Eva!" The command is there in his tone now, and blistering anger.

I've never actually seen him angry before—at least not with me. Even that first night, when his car was damaged, his anger wasn't really directed at me. Now it is, and it's terrifying. All the more so for having erupted out of almost nowhere. A chance remark, an innocent question, and suddenly my fragile composure disintegrates. Is everything in my life really so flimsy?

But even the blast of Nathan's anger is not as terrifying as the truth. The dreadful, humiliating, reality of why I left Oxford, why I ran so hard and so fast and never dared look back. And it's not just the utter shame of what happened to me back then—it's also the impact it could have on the here and now. Always, throughout everything we've done together, Nathan has insisted on informed consent. Almost to the point of obsession he's made his requirements clear, made sure I understood. The whole thing rested, surely, on both of us being 'of sound mind'. What will he make of my so-called consent now, once he finds out I'm a flake? Will he still believe I knew what I was doing, what I was agreeing to? Maybe not. Probably not.

So now I've no alternative but to lie, evade, defy him.

"Nothing! Nothing happened. I left. I'd had enough, couldn't stand it there anymore. I needed to get out. So I left. Not that it's got anything to do with you." All my defences are on high alert, and the more I resist the more his suspicions are well and truly aroused. I've seen him persistent before, but never so brutally relentless. He's on the trail of something. I know what it is, he only thinks he does. But he's filling in the blanks for himself. Putting two and two together and making five.

"Ah yes, your emotional car crash. I'd forgotten about that. And as long as you're tutoring my daughter, staying in my home, everything about you is my business. So, what happened in Oxford? And if not back there, where will you go when your contract here ends?"

Pushing away from him I manage to wrench my arm free, or maybe he decides to relinquish his grip. I scoot down to the far end of the settee. My arms folded tightly across my chest, I glare defensively at him, defiant and desperate to head him off. No way am I discussing my work at Oxford, my old life. No way is he getting anywhere even close to my breakdown. Not a sniff. The taint of mental illness is behind me, it's not a part of who I am now, where I am now. That's all in the past—it *is* because I say it is. I'm here now and starting over.

Made reckless by fear and desperation I toss my defiance back at him. "Oxford's got nothing to do with you so just leave it. And I'm going nowhere. I'm staying here. Well, Black Combe, or thereabouts. There, I mean. This is my home."

"Fuck that. What the hell are you on about? You said you'd never been here, there, before?" He is clearly bewildered, and to be fair that does make two of us. I try to explain myself.

"As soon as I looked out that first morning, and I saw the moors, I felt I… Well, I felt I recognised the place. That I belonged there. It seemed like home. And that feeling has just got stronger over the last couple of weeks. More compelling. I've walked the moors with Rosie. And Barney. And I love it. I think I'll always love it. So I want to stay. I want to stay in Yorkshire, stay on the Brontë moors. I love Black Combe. I've made some friends already—you, Rosie, Mrs Richardson. Even your friend Tom seems nice. Me and Rosie went up the Greystones and he showed me round the farm. So… I've decided I want to stay here, find work. Settle down."

He is silent, staring at me in disbelief. And he is angry. So very, very angry. Even I, emotional cripple that I am, can sense the tension, the sudden chill. Why didn't I keep my big mouth shut?

"So, you're intending to stay. Permanently. At Black Combe. At my home? You're moving in. Just like that."

"No, I only meant…" I had never intended to outstay my welcome at Black Combe. I was thinking of looking around for somewhere to rent, but he's not listening. His tone is biting, his posture stiff as he stands, looming over me. Without thinking I cringe away, making myself small as I huddle on the settee.

"Stop that. I'm not going to fucking hit you, even if you do deserve it."

He is obviously furious, disgusted with me. And I am genuinely at a loss. What's brought this on? I only said I wanted to move into his neighbourhood, for Christ's sake!

"Please, I didn't mean…"

"I've heard enough. Enough lies and half-truths. Enough evasion and bloody mystery. I need to know who's around my daughter, and I'm sick of trying to work you out. Last chance, Eva. Why can't you go back to Oxford?"

Desperately miserable, I curl up into a ball. Why couldn't he just let it lie? "I can't, that's all. It's nothing, not like you think anyway…"

"Right, I've heard enough. Now shut up and get out."

"What? What do you mean?" I feel the tears spring to my eyes. How did this happen? "Why? What have I done? Don't you trust me?" Am I pleading with him? Maybe. I'm no good at this stuff. If this is 'doing relationships' it's not what it's cracked up to be.

"Trust you? Why the fucking hell would I trust you? I ask you a few straight questions and you lie through your teeth and tell me to mind my own business. And as for moving in, it's manners to wait until you're asked. I didn't invite you to move in. You're my sub, that's all. My *current* sub. I like fucking you well enough, but I'm not looking for a soulmate. So I want you out. Out of here. Out of Black Combe." With one last withering look at me huddling on his settee, cowering in silence, he heads for the door.

"I'm going out. I'll be back by six, and I want you gone by then. You. And all your stuff. Gone. Is that clear? *Is that clear?*"

I don't answer. There's no need. No room for negotiation, for apology, for any further argument.

This is me getting dumped. Big style. I hear the door slam and know I'm alone. As before. As usual. As always.

I sit in stunned silence for a while. I've got three hours so no real hurry. It won't take me more than a few minutes to gather my stuff together, so I allow myself the luxury of wallowing in my grief.

I've never really thought about what 'heartbroken' might feel like, but I guess this is it. This feeling of rejection, betrayal, injustice. And of loss, emptiness. And, above all, loneliness. He might be a jerk, a heartless, intolerant bastard, but I did manage to somehow fall in love with him. And now he's gone. He's left me, dumped me, because I'm a freak. A bloody stupid, mentally unstable freak who couldn't keep her mouth shut. And who couldn't, wouldn't take the risk of just telling him the truth.

I didn't need to have that conversation about settling in Yorkshire at all. All I needed to do was book into a hotel at the end of my contract and there would have been nothing he could have done about it. He might even have been pleased I was staying, if we'd got on well, if I'd continued to be a good lay. But now, he just hates me. And I genuinely have no idea why. No idea what I did or said that was so wrong. He has his secrets, his privacy, and I respect that. And I'm entitled to mine, surely. If I came on too strong, too soon, it was a genuine mistake. I never meant to assume anything. And above all, breakdown or not, I'm perfectly safe to leave alone with his daughter, and in his heart he must know that.

I may be a lot of things, but stupid is not one of them. This is just an excuse. An excuse to dump me, to get rid before I become too clingy. He was looking for an exit route and I handed it to him. And now, it's over.

Desperately wishing I could rewind, take us back to the easy companionship and passionate lovemaking of just a half-hour ago, I eventually force myself into action. I need to pack. My shredded pride tells me I need to not be here when he comes back. My head aching from crying, I push myself to my feet, giving myself stern lectures about pulling myself together, and make my way to the guest room where my new clothes are still piled on the bed.

Half an hour later I am ready. Dressed in a smart, black mid-calf-length skirt and plum-red wrap-around top, and defiantly wearing my fuck-me red heels, I drag my bags towards the door. I've called down and my taxi should be at the front entrance in a few minutes so I'd like to get all my gear downstairs. Why didn't I think to buy a proper case? I curse as I balance carrier bags in a pile by the lift.

I turn to fetch the last couple of bags and I'm startled by the low swishing hum as the lift doors open. I glance back in surprise, and Nathan is there. He strides through the sliding doors, glancing sharply at my precarious heap of Harvey Nicks bags as he makes straight for me.

Three hours. He'd said I had three hours. He said he wouldn't be back until six. Surely I've not taken too long...

I back away, not wanting to be on the receiving end of more of his contempt. Maybe I can just shove my stuff into the lift and go...

"You're still here."

"Yes, but I'm just..."

"Thank God. I'm sorry, Eva. Please don't go. Don't leave me."

Before I can answer he is on me, lifting me, carrying me back into his apartment. Kicking the door shut behind us. I am slammed against the wall and he is kissing me. Desperately, hungrily. His tongue is thrust into my mouth, my throat. His hands are in my hair, holding my head still for his assault. He still hasn't shaved and his bristly chin scratches my face, my neck. My hands on his shoulders I try to find balance as he lifts me off my feet.

Totally confused by this U-turn, and more than a bit pissed off at his blowing hot and cold like this, I try to get my hands between us to push him away. Who the hell does he think he is, to treat me like something he found under his shoe one minute and try to lick my tonsils the next? I may be crap at relationships, but even I know I deserved a chance to explain, to defend myself. He just lost his temper, for no good reason that I can see, and ordered me out of his home. Sacked me from a job I love, a job I'm good at. And now he seems to think he can just waltz back in and kiss me senseless, and it'll all be all right again. No bloody chance!

I manage to get some purchase on his shoulders and shove hard. It's nowhere near enough to dislodge him, but I do manage to get my message across that I'm not having this. Not doing this. He ends the kiss, lifting his head to murmur in my ear.

"Eva, sweetheart, I'm sorry. Truly. Please…"

It's enough, feeble, needy creature that I am—that I seem to become around Nathan Darke. I give up the struggle.

His mouth hardly parts from mine as I am carried to his bedroom and dropped on the bed. "You're wearing new clothes again, Eva, and you look absolutely gorgeous. Take them off."

I stare at him, no longer afraid—after all, I am familiar enough with this side of Nathan Darke—but I'm totally confused. Does he want me, still? Am I to stay after all? Do I want to?

"Your clothes, Eva. Please?"

Yes. I do want to. Wordlessly I strip, and lie back.

"Is this to be my punishment fuck then?" I whisper the words, hoping that once he's done we can, perhaps, somehow, get back to how we were before.

"No, Eva. It's a forgive me fuck. I'm a stupid, heartless bastard, and I want you to forgive me. Let me try again. Can you do that?"

"I... Yes, yes, I can. And I don't need to forgive you. It was me, my fault. There's no need for this. Really, Nathan, it's okay. We need to talk, not..."

"We'll talk later. For now, let me do this. For you. Just shut up, lie back and enjoy it."

Kneeling beside the bed he grabs my legs and pulls me towards him, spreading my thighs wide. His mouth is on me, and I stop thinking, stop trying to work out what's going on. He flicks my clit with his tongue then slips it into my vagina. I can feel his stubble, abrasive against my tender skin. Usually clean-shaven, this is a new and exciting sensation. He tongue-fucks me until I am moaning with pleasure, then suddenly he slips his hands under my bottom, lifting me up. He uses his tongue to rim my anus, and I scream. The pleasure is overwhelming. Quite, quite exquisite. Holding me in place with one hand, easily, he brings his other hand round to stroke my eager clitoris and I am lost. I come, fast and hard, gasping his name as the sensations burst through me, bolts of lightning streaking out through my fingers and toes. I am convulsing wildly, out of control, as he relentlessly works me with his mouth, his tongue, his fingers.

Even as the orgasm subsides he isn't done. He continues to work on me, his thumb now sliding in and out of my pussy as he gently nips my clitoris, taking it between his lips to suck me, hard. Incredibly, my arousal spikes again, and within moments I am caught up, tossed around in a second orgasmic tsunami. I am thrashing on the bed, nearly mindless with pleasure, and still he continues, relentlessly dragging a third climax from me.

Exhausted at last, I need to stop. It's too much. I can't take any more. And I remember.

"Red. Red. Please stop," I whisper, my limbs weak, my breath catching in my throat. He hears me. And he stops.

"Enough, sweetheart? Am I forgiven?" The gentle question is whispered, soft, compassionate. Caring.

"Yes, enough. And I told you there's no need for forgiving." I lie still for a few seconds, just breathing, my senses returning. Then, my heart rate returning to something nearer normal, I continue. "God, that was incredible. The best ever. But my head's a mess. I need to rest, I need to recover. And, soon, we need to talk."

He lifts his head, looks into my eyes, smiles that sweet, sexy smile, and slides up onto the bed to lie next to me. And I realise he's still fully dressed. As ever it seems, at my moments of greatest weakness, greatest vulnerability, he is fully dressed and I'm naked.

"Overdressed as usual, Mr Darke," I mutter grumpily.

"Force of habit, Miss Byrne."

"That's Dr Byrne to you."

"Ah yes, Dr Byrne. I'm trying."

"Very." And I turn to snuggle against him as his arm comes round me, holding me tightly against his chest, draped bonelessly across him. And, again, I sleep.

Chapter Five

"Get your bloody clothes off!"

I don't honestly care whether we're both naked or both fully clothed, but there's no way I'm going to even attempt a serious conversation with our respective states of dress—or undress—so unbalanced.

He doesn't move to oblige me, so I punch him in the ribs. "Either you get naked or I get dressed. And then, only then, do we talk."

"Jesus, Eva. You're just too fucking bossy to make a decent sub. Christ knows what I ever saw in you." Grumbling to himself, he quickly gets his shirt off, soon followed by his jeans and shorts. I note somewhat in passing that his erection is still pretty impressive, or maybe that's more or less his permanent state. Or maybe it's just his usual state around me—what a lovely thought. Quite encouraging really.

Throwing himself back down alongside me, he's still grumbling. "Bloody women, never satisfied."

"Oh, I'm perfectly satisfied. For now. I'll let you know when I'm not." The worm is turning, it seems. Nathan seems to approve because he is kissing me. Again. At last he raises his head to look into my eyes, and rubs his nose against mine playfully.

"I was so scared you'd have left already. Scared I might not get back in time to stop you. Christ. I might never have found you again. I don't even have your address in London."

"My mother's address. Remember. And you could have found me through the agency. But anyway, I wasn't going to London. I was going to Black Combe." I run my fingers through his long, soft, gorgeous hair and at his start of surprise I decide to put him out of his misery. "For my violin and the rest of my stuff. And then I was going to look for somewhere to rent. Like I said, I'm staying. In Yorkshire."

"You don't need a place to rent. You have somewhere to stay. Black Combe."

I push myself up on one elbow to look down at him, more than a little taken aback. "Only until the end of my contract, strictly speaking. That's about three more weeks. Are you suggesting I stay on? Why? Earlier you seemed so dead set against me moving in."

He reaches up to run the backs of his fingers down my cheek, tucking a stray lock of hair behind my ear. "Not move in exactly, well not like you might think. It's awkward, Eva." Slipping his hand to the back of my neck he tightens his hold as I begin to pull away, not wanting to hear him tell me again that he doesn't want me, or at least that he doesn't want me there. In his home.

"Just listen, will you?" He pulls me back down, tight up against his chest. "Black Combe is Rosie's home. I'm her father. She needs safety, security. She needs to know she can always trust me, that she comes first with me. That's just how it has to be with kids. So, I never take women, girlfriends, there. Never."

"No Dom-sub stuff at Black Combe then?" I ask innocently. "No whips or canes? No nipple clamps? No butt plugs?"

"God, no!"

"Pity, could have been interesting. But I understand the situation, so, that's agreed. I'm so glad we got that clear. And I'm assuming no girlfriend stuff either? No kissing? No cuddling? No stripping me to the waist and sucking my nipples until I have an orgasm on the kitchen table?"

"Shit, Eva, that was different."

I giggle. He's so easy to wind up sometimes. "Calm down, idiot. I care about Rosie too. I know we need to be discreet. And I somehow think I'm going to be better at discretion than you. I'm Miss Inhibitions 2012 remember?"

He pats my bum, and I get the distinct impression he's thinking of doing rather more. I need to go easy on the teasing. For now, though, he's fine. We're fine. "Yeah, you probably will be. Discreet's your middle name, Miss Byrne."

"And there's such a lot in a name, with you, isn't there?"

"Excuse me?"

"My name. Or rather, names. You have different names for me according to what I am. At that moment. What I am to you. And how you are feeling, how you want me to feel…"

Glancing up I can see his genuine bewilderment written all over his gorgeous face. "What are you talking about, Eva?"

"Ah, so now I'm Eva. Eva's my girlfriend name. Or when we're out in public. You call me Eva when you're angry too, or being serious like now. I'm not sure I always like being Eva." He's silent, waiting, still at a total loss it would seem, so I continue.

"Miss Byrne, or Dr Byrne when you remember, is my teacher name. That's what you call me at home, at Black Combe. And it's my sub name. You always call me Miss Byrne when you have a whip in your hand." I shudder involuntarily. "Miss Byrne is the me you hurt. And often she's the me you fuck, especially when it's not the gentle sort of fucking. Being Miss Byrne scares me. And excites me too."

I hear his muffled "Christ" in my hair, but there's more I need, want to say.

"And then there's Angel. I love being Angel. Angel is the me you like, really like, really care for. Like my dad did. And you call me Angel when we make love, when you come. And sometimes when I come. And that's not like my dad. That's just you."

I wait, silently, for him to respond.

"Jesus, Eva…"

"Eva?"

"Eva. Miss Byrne. Angel. You're clearly a woman of many parts, sweetheart. And too damned bright for me, I reckon. Okay, so you got me sussed on all that name stuff. And while we're on the super-sensitives, having this little heart to heart, are you going to tell me now about Oxford? About why you left?"

I stiffen, my heart plummeting as I get ready to do battle again, but he just drops it this time, goes on. "No? Okay then, if we're not going to discuss the past let's talk about the future. About your plans. You'll be living at Black Combe, that's settled. As some sort of girlfriend, no doubt—we'll have to work that out.

With Rosie. But what about work? Somehow I can't see you being satisfied doing nothing for long. And with all your many and various qualifications you're not going to be looking for a job in Oakworth bread shop."

"I like bread."

"Eva." His warning growl suggests I need to get serious. And, in fairness, I have been giving this some thought.

"Okay, I could teach. I need to get a teaching qualification to work in a school, but that shouldn't be a problem. Like I say, qualifications come easy to me. Or I could do more private tuition — maths, music, languages. Or I could do translations."

Rolling onto his back, one arm around me, the other behind his head, he's obviously thinking about my prospects. "Hmm, I don't know about the teaching stuff, not my field, but I'd say there's a market for interpretation and translation in business, especially if your mathematics skills can be applied to commercial accountancy and finance. I'd employ you."

"You'd just spend all your time fucking me in your office, or bending me over your conference table if I got my sums wrong. I'm not working for you!"

His low chuckle and gentle caress across my breasts suggest to me I'm right not to contemplate joining Darke Associates as a serious career move, but maybe there's a niche in the business world I could fill. It's a new direction for me, but might be worth considering...

He tips my chin up with his finger to hold my gaze, serious again. "Well I've got a use for your Turkish as we've already established. But apart from helping out me and Ahmet, I suspect there's not a great deal of demand for Turkish. Do you speak any other languages, Eva?"

"Yes, one or two." My guarded tone seems to have caught his interest and he's probing.

"Well, which is it? One? Or two? Or more, perhaps?" My dropped gaze gives me away—he knows I'm evading and he's on it straight away. "More then. It *is* more, isn't it? Which languages do you speak? Come on, Eva, spill."

"French. And German." He says nothing, just waiting. He knows there's more. "Turkish, obviously. And Russian."

"Russian? Interesting choice. Any more? Eva?"

Resigned I roll onto my back, staring up at the ceiling. "Fluently? Those I mentioned already, plus Mandarin Chinese, Spanish, Arabic, Polish, Italian and Greek. I'm also reasonably proficient in Latin and Ancient Greek. And I can get by in probably a couple of dozen other languages, if I have to."

The silence in the room is deafening, broken at last by a low whistle. "Shit, that's some repertoire, Miss Byrne." Now he's the one leaning up on one elbow, looking down at me, and he waits until I turn my head to meet his gaze. "How'd you ever get the time to learn all those? And why bother?"

"Why? Because I just can. And it doesn't take long. I just have an aptitude for it, I suppose, it comes naturally, very little effort required. And some languages are very similar to others—French, Italian, Spanish, for example. You learn one, you learn 'em all."

"I think you undersell your skills, Miss Byrne. You just rattled off—what was it nine, ten different languages you claim to be fluent in? As well as English."

"What do you mean 'claim'? I bloody well am!"

"I know, I know, don't get your knickers in a twist. So to speak…"

More stroking and patting my bare bum and I let my hackles settle back down again.

He continues, his tone serious now. "I didn't mean that. I know you're bloody brilliant and I believe you can do anything you set your mind to, quite frankly. So, what's your method for learning languages? Do you join a class? Go live abroad for a while? What?"

"Both. I learnt French and German at school originally, but only really became fluent by going to those countries. I learnt Greek and Turkish by spending a month in Cyprus."

"A month? You mastered two separate languages in a month?"

"Like I said. Aptitude. I developed verbal fluency first, then literacy. Turkish and Greek both use different alphabets from English so it's more complicated. Same goes for Russian and Mandarin. And Arabic, obviously. For me it's always verbal first, then the written form." I stop, peeping up at him to see how he's taking all this. His face is a mask of wonder. He shakes his head slowly, but still says nothing. Suddenly it's important to me that I try to explain, make him understand.

"When I'm starting from scratch, a completely new language like, say, Urdu would be to me, I start by reading up on the grammatical rules, the syntax, so I know the theory of it. Then I sort of collect the vocabulary, usually through the international media. I think of it as harvesting. I find listening to native speakers is much better than formal language training, at least for me. Once I get the first few words and phrases sorted out the rest is easy. I start to build my frame of reference and it just falls into place from there. I fill in the gaps from what I hear, and as my vocabulary builds up I apply the grammatical rules I learnt at the beginning of the process."

"But if you don't understand any of it, how do you start? And how can you remember all the grammar right from the beginning. And apply it correctly? Don't you need a teacher, someone to practise on?" He is frowning, bewildered, and in fairness to me it really is very difficult to explain all this to someone with no linguistic training. But I'm determined to try.

"There are some words that are more or less universal. That means they appear in just about every language in more or less unchanged form. Often they're technical words such as 'telephone', 'airport', or maybe to do with travel and tourism such as 'taxi', and 'hotel'. Those words always leap out at me, and from them, well, the phrases they appear in really – I can usually identify the definite and indefinite articles. That's 'the' and 'a' in English, and the conjunctives such as 'but', and 'and'."

I realise I'm getting technical and stop, chewing my lip nervously. Trust me to go off on one and get boring. It's the stargazing night all over again.

"Go on, Eva. I think I'm following you so far." I risk a peep, and his eyes certainly don't have that bored, glazed look I'm so used to seeing when I try to explain my 'talent'. "How do you get from there to being a fluent speaker? And can you always do it in a month?"

"Easily, if I don't have any distractions. And it's not just speaking. I do reading and writing too as a rule. I just tune my TV, radio or whatever into the right broadcaster and listen in, absorbing the vocabulary and usage. It helps if I don't hear or need to use any other language during that period, if I can focus my undivided attention. Within a few hours it starts dropping into place, and within days I'm there. And when I've mastered the verbal fluency I usually tackle the written form. But really, once you know a language, reading it is just a matter of decoding print. An unfamiliar alphabet is a challenge, but it's just a matter of learning it, assigning sounds to symbols. Simple phonetics really."

"Doesn't sound remotely simple to me. It's bloody amazing. And something tells me you've done this little caper of yours a lot more than just ten times to have got it to such a fine art. So, honestly now, Eva — how many languages do you have? Not fluent necessarily, but workable, a functioning ability?"

"I don't know." At his grunt of exasperated disbelief I rush on. I want him to believe me. "Really, I don't. I don't bother to count. But, I suppose it's loads. Dozens." My voice small, I hesitate, wondering what he's going to make of this, of me, now. "So there you have it — I'm the nerdy little specky four-eyed creep who sits at the back of the class. The one whose homework always gets copied but no one invites home for tea, who never gets invited to birthday parties."

"Loads. Yeah, I'll bet it's loads. And I prefer to describe you as my sexy little boffin. You know, Eva, clever women are a real turn-on for most men. Definitely for this one. And you're one seriously clever woman so stop hiding down there, blushing like the little virgin we both know you're not. Well, not any longer anyway. Hold your head up and be proud of what you can do." Sitting up, he pulls me up to kneel in front of him, and reaching for a box of tissues beside the bed he wipes my face. "Stop crying, love, there's no need to cry. Not over this anyway. And just for the record, I reckon you'll have no trouble at all making a living, here in Yorkshire or anywhere else in the world. You're an international superstar. A human Babel fish."

"A what?"

"Ah, your not too classical education didn't stretch to *The Hitchhiker's Guide* then? I'll lend you my copy. But seriously, from what you say, you could go anywhere in the world, anywhere at all, and within hours be understanding the language and start to make yourself understood. This 'gift' of yours is gold dust. It really is. Not just because of the commercial applications—what about the military uses, and international diplomacy. You, young lady, are a highly merchantable commodity."

I'm not convinced. "I'm a freak. Some sort of curiosity. In the old days I'd have been in a circus, or burnt as a witch."

"Well, think yourself lucky this is the twenty-first century then. We're enlightened." Then, in one of his mercurial mood changes, he drops back down to make himself comfortable against the pillows. "And just because you're such a boffin, and I'm such an enlightened child of the twenty-first century, don't think you're getting out of making the tea. It's your turn. I take one sugar. And don't forget the Bourbons."

"Chauvinist..." I dump the box of tissues on his chest as I grin and slide off the bed starting to hunt around for my clothes.

"Naked, Eva. We both stay naked, remember. We're not done talking yet. So do be careful not to splash."

So, gloriously, unashamedly nude, I go to put the kettle on.

* * * *

"Can I ask you something?"

We're both sitting cross-legged on the bed, a tray of tea and biscuits between us on the duvet. It seems totally natural to be chatting to Nathan while he rakes his appreciative gaze across my naked breasts, my belly, my smooth, hairless and highly visible pussy. I'm doing my own share of admiring too—he really does have an amazing body. Hard, sculpted, athletic, finely honed pectorals and a six-pack to match. His erection is jutting at me and I long to take it in my hands, or maybe my mouth, stroke his shaft, cup his balls... I know it won't be long before we make love again, but first, I'd like to satisfy my curiosity. And feed my insecurities.

He glances at me, quickly swallows the last of his Bourbon biscuit before mumbling his reply, "Mmm, what?"

"Can I ask you about your wife?"

"My wife? What wife?"

"Your wife. Rosie's mother. I suppose..." I take a deep breath. "I suppose you must have loved her very much..."

He hesitates. At first I think he's going to refuse to answer me at all. Then, "No. Not really."

"But she was your wife. You were married to her. You must have loved her."

"She—Louisa—*was* my wife, briefly. I liked her. I cared about her. I was sorry when she died. But I didn't love her."

This is beyond me. "But you adopted her child. I don't understand..."

"I loved Rosie. I always have. Adopting her was a no-brainer when Louisa died."

"But…"

"It's complicated, Eva."

"So is my linguistic ability, but I tried to explain it to you. I'm beginning to think this disclosure thing is very one-way."

"Fair point, I suppose, but this is personal, Eva. Private."

I arch an unimpressed eyebrow. "Oh really, like that ever stops you…!"

"Okay, okay, I'll tell you about Louisa. But this is confidential, sensitive. Rosie knows some of it but not all. You'll understand why soon enough. I need you to promise me you'll respect my wishes on this, love."

I nod, and after carefully placing the tray on the floor beside the bed I lie down next to Nathan who is arranging the pillows behind us. He holds out an arm and I snuggle into him.

"Louisa was my sub. Occasionally."

I couldn't have been more surprised if he'd told me his dead wife was Mother Teresa and Princess Diana rolled into one. "Your sub. A sub—like me? You married a sub!"

"Well, not quite like you. Louisa was a damned good sub and you, sweetheart, are simply not. You're sexy and exciting and bloody lovely. Most of the time. But submissive—hardly. You do try hard, though, and you have other obvious attractions so I put up with you." He tips my chin up to plant a quick kiss on my mouth, his tender smile and warm gaze emphasising the irony of his words, before he continues drily, "And you do get full marks for effort."

I can't help smiling back, but I'm not being sidetracked by compliments. "You married a sub? How? Why?"

With a sigh, he rolls me onto my back and kisses me again, properly this time. His tongue swoops into my mouth and after a few moments I stop resisting and let him have his way. For now. He deepens the kiss, sliding his hands over my body. He circles my nipples with his fingers, swallowing my gasps as arousal starts to spike. He lifts his head, gazing down into my eyes. "Like I said, sexy, exciting and bloody lovely. Now, are you going to shut up and listen, at least pretend to be a half-decent sub?"

I nod, smiling, and he rolls onto his back, staring up at the ceiling.

"Louisa liked it rough. Very rough. She loved to be beaten. Hard, and for a long, long time. She was exhausting. Stamina like an ox, and I guess a hide like one as well." And with a nudge to my ribs, he continues, "She never fainted when I caned her, and I don't recall she ever safe worded either."

"Good for her," I mutter.

"What was that, Miss Byrne?"

"Nothing. Go on."

"Thank you, Miss Byrne. As I was saying, I first met Louisa when she was about seven months pregnant with Rosie. Her usual Dom wasn't interested in anything not involving bondage, and even Louisa realised that being strapped down and whipped when heavily pregnant was not a wise move. As she couldn't manage to get her usual supplier to engage in anything even remotely vanilla she'd been doing without sex for a while. She was frustrated and desperate when she contacted me through an online contacts agency and suggested we get together for some not-so-gentle fucking. As you might have noticed, my tastes are a little more...flexible and I could deliver the intensity Louisa was after without the brutality. We spent a very enjoyable afternoon and evening together, and after her baby — Rosie — was born she took up where she'd left off with her usual guy. I didn't see her again for months."

"It all sounds very...casual. Are all your relationships like that?"

"Yes, more or less. Until now."

I smile to myself. That sounded good.

"Louisa and I got together a couple of times during the next year or so, and it was always a lot of fun. But bloody knackering. I couldn't have done with her on a regular basis. One time I ran into her by accident. She was having a coffee in Starbucks, downstairs on the ground floor here. I'd called in for a latte on my way home, and there she was, with Rosie asleep in a pushchair. That was the first time I ever saw Rosie and I think she was about six months old or so then. I sat with her, them. We had a coffee, then another, and I invited her up to the apartment."

"What about the baby?"

"Well, obviously I invited her too."

"What, to watch?"

"Bloody hell, Eva, you've got a dirty mind. Of course not to watch. Jeez. No, we called in at Tesco Express, picked up a pack of disposable nappies, some formula milk and a jar of baby food, and came up here. Louisa fed Rosie, changed her nappy, and we played with her and watched TV until she fell asleep. Then Louisa settled her in the guest bedroom — the one you've been using for your clothes — and we...got started on our evening's entertainment. Afterwards Louisa was dead to the world, fast asleep in my bed. I think by now you know how exhausting it is, especially for the sub. So when Rosie started crying at about three in the morning, Louisa never stirred. And rather than disturb her I went to see what was up.

"Rosie was awake, and pretty miserable. She was in a strange place, I guess, her nappy was wet and I think she must have been hungry too. I fed her, changed her, tickled her tummy a bit because she seemed to like that. And then I took her into bed with us. She soon fell asleep again. But I was in love. She was the cutest, sweetest little thing. I adored her. In the morning I persuaded Louisa to let me feed her again, and then they left.

"It would have been about eighteen months later when I saw Louisa again. She and her regular Dom had had a falling out and she was at a loose end, so she decided to look me up. That time was when I noticed the lump in her breast."

He stops, his eyes still fixed on the ceiling, swallows a couple of times before continuing. Clearly this is a painful memory and I start to wonder if I should have just left it all alone.

"I told her, obviously. And urged her to see her doctor. After all, it might not be anything serious. Anyway, she did. And it was. Serious I mean. Serious and malignant. And aggressive. Not that she bothered to tell me any of that. Months went by and I didn't hear anything from her. Obviously I wondered how she had gone on, but she wasn't answering my calls or texts. In fairness, I didn't give her a lot of thought, but one day I was in South Leeds, near where she lived, so I decided on a little social call. I was curious, and I suppose a bit concerned. I knew she had a flat in a tower block in Cottingley so I went round there. I got a neighbour to let me into the block and I went up, hammered on her door. It was ages before she answered. I'd have thought she was out and I might have left it, but I could hear a child—Rosie—crying, so I waited and carried on knocking. And eventually she opened the door.

"She looked awful. Haggard. She was obviously very ill. She'd had the first lot of surgery, and some chemo, which had perhaps slowed things down a bit. But it had come back. With a vengeance. It came back and from then the cancer developed so fast. Christ, even now I can't believe how fast it spread. Louisa was just starting her second bout of chemo when I came banging on her door. And she was so alone. Except for Rosie, of course, but she was in no shape to look after herself let alone a toddler. I just shoved the pair of them in my car and brought them back here."

I don't know which is greater in that moment, my surprise or my admiration. The great, intimidating, stern Nathan Darke has his lighter side. His caring for the sick side. Who knew?

"How did you manage? A sick woman and a small child?"

"It wasn't easy. I'd only just moved in here and just started Darke Associates so I was working all hours. I spent as much time with Louisa as I could, but it wasn't enough. Wouldn't have been anywhere near enough without Grace. Grace—Mrs Richardson—was working for me then as my cook-cum-housekeeper. She had a small apartment on the floor below and she helped me. A lot. With Louisa and with Rosie. I hired a nurse for Louisa, and a nanny for Rosie, and Grace sort of oversaw everything. She was brilliant and I'll never forget it.

"There was never going to be a good outcome, though, we all knew that. Louisa was a fighter, and she struggled to fight the disease. At first, maybe, there was a bit of improvement—as much to do with being cared for, properly fed, as anything else. But really, she deteriorated fast. All told, she was only here for about eight months. She died more or less two years to the day from me first spotting that bloody lump."

He stops, again gathering his thoughts, reliving what must have been the most harrowing experience I can ever start to imagine. And I'd thought I'd had a challenging time. God, this certainly puts my stuff into perspective.

"Louisa tried so hard to fight the cancer—she desperately wanted to live. For her little girl. But she knew. She knew she wasn't going to make it. She saw Rosie turn three—we had a party round her bed—but she knew she wouldn't see Rosie's fourth birthday, or spend another Christmas with her. I knew it too. So did Grace. And we knew we had to sort out Rosie's future. I'd asked Louisa if there was anyone, any family she wanted me to contact for her, but there really was no one. Her parents were dead. She was an only child.

"Then, one day, out of the blue, she asked me to adopt Rosie. To promise I'd look after her after Louisa was gone. It was the only solution, the obvious solution. And I loved Rosie. I'd always loved her since she was a baby and I got up to see to her in the night. So I thanked Louisa for her wonderful, cherished gift to me, and agreed. It was a no-brainer.

"We married a few days later, here, with Grace and the nurse as witnesses and Rosie as our bridesmaid. I bought Rosie a beautiful dress and she loved it. She has it still. I legally adopted Rosie on our wedding day so there could be no uncertainty when the time came. I was her stepfather, her legally adopted father. It was a done deal. Louisa died two weeks later."

"Nathan. Oh God, Nathan." Turning to him I just want to hold him. I can think of nothing to say. Nothing I might ever have imagined came close to this reality. This astonishing, profound generosity in the face of such utter tragedy.

"It's okay, love. It was a long time ago. We came through it. Me, Rosie and Grace even. We came through it together. I'd acquired Black Combe about a year earlier. A client of mine commissioned me to design a scheme for him to turn it into holiday lets, but his finance fell through and he had to back out. I really liked the place, though, and thought the scheme was a winner so I bought the property at auction. I originally intended to convert it for holiday lets as per my original design but, like I told you before, when I realised I was going to need a family home I decided Black Combe was it. So I redid my designs, turned it into the place you see now. It took about six months, but we moved there as soon as we could.

"I asked the nanny to stay on, but she was a city girl, didn't fancy the wilds of Oakworth and I can't really blame her I suppose. But Grace surprised me. I never expected her to come with us, but she did. She upped and moved with us, to look after the house, and Rosie. And Rosie had always wanted a dog. She begged and pleaded, and I thought it would be nice for her to have some company so we went to the Dogs Trust to find a nice rescue mutt. And met Barney. Rosie took one look and it was love at first sight."

"I bet you got a shock when your cuddly puppy grew into a donkey."

"He was about eighteen months old and fully grown when we met him so I knew what I was getting. He'd been there a few months already — not many people can find space for a dog that size. Or afford to feed one. But Black Combe is perfect for him. And he fitted straight in. No interest in sheep, thank God, so he and Rosie can roam the moors as much as they like. And I don't worry about her when she's with the dog. I can always find her if I need to."

"What, because he's so big you can see him from outer space?"

"Not exactly. I had a tracking sensor fitted to his collar. I can track him from my laptop or iPad, and where Barney is, so will Rosie be."

I'm not sure if I find his methods of keeping tabs on his daughter shocking or brilliant, but opt for the former. "Bloody control freak..."

"I prefer concerned parent, but whatever you say..." Rolling to his side, he looks down at me, wanting me to understand, approve. Now he knows how I feel most of the time...

"Seriously, I didn't move out to the wilds of Oakworth just so Rosie could stay indoors, nice and safe inside. I want her to be out there, enjoying her world, and this is a way of making it safe for her, more or less. There've been lots of times I've had to go out on the quad and fetch her home as it drops dark, and if I'd no idea where she was I'd be frantic. And at least a couple of times she'd have been out on the moors on her own after dark if I hadn't known where to find her, which is a definite no-no. So, this works, everyone's happy." He looks hesitant. "Do you really think I'm weird?"

"Hey, how would I know? And anyway, I've cornered the market on weird."

"A bit quirky, maybe, but not weird. Well, not very weird..."

As I aim a retaliatory punch into his ribs, he rolls off me, his feet hit the floor and he is away, grabbing his jeans from the floor. He pauses in the doorway, turns back to me.

"We missed Tennessee Williams with all your soul-searching and navel-gazing and digging into my murky past, but that's no reason to starve. When did you last eat anything apart from chocolate Bourbons?"

My tummy gives a helpful little growl by way of indicating he may be onto something.

He smiles. "Thought so. Give me half an hour to sort out some food."

"Should I dress for dinner?" I call out, halting him once more as he heads out of the door.

"Only if you can manage black tie. And nothing else." He winks as he closes the bedroom door behind him.

Chapter Six

I carefully put the finishing touches to an artful Windsor knot, tugging it tight around my neck and making sure the two ends of the black silk tie I found hanging on the rack inside Nathan's wardrobe door hang nice and straight between my breasts. It's important to get the tie just so I think, because it's all I'm wearing. In true, obedient sub style, I am otherwise completely naked. Satisfied, I make my way out of the bedroom, following my nose in pursuit of some mouthwatering smells. Hopefully I won't run into a spotty pizza delivery boy out there.

Nathan is alone, thankfully, his back to me as he fiddles with something on the gas hob. He is wearing his blue denim jeans from earlier, and an untucked, unbuttoned light grey shirt. He appears to be cooking. I didn't expect that.

Suddenly self-conscious at my near-as-makes-no-difference nudity I start to retreat back into the bedroom, but he turns. Obviously he heard me come in. He whistles and looks me up and down, his lustful expression unmistakable. Any second now I'm going to find myself flung on my back and soundly fucked, which is a nice idea, but really, I'd like to eat first.

Nathan apparently feels the same way. "Nice outfit. The tie will come in useful later, as a blindfold. Or maybe I'll just tie you up with it. Now, sit down, make yourself comfortable. Here's a little light reading to keep you occupied while I finish making your dinner." He gestures to a tall stool alongside the worktop close to where he's busy at the stove, and slides his iPad along the counter in front of me. I pick it up and press the 'on' switch, half expecting some more bondage paraphernalia to appear. But no, it's an e-book reader app, displaying the title page of Douglas Adams' *Hitchhikers Guide to the Galaxy*.

"You'll find the Babel fish in chapter ten I think, but start from the beginning. You'll love it." He turns back to the stove, and wordlessly I start to read.

He's right. I absolutely do love it, the zany, quirky, clever humour mixing the gloriously improbable with the numbingly mundane. Before long I'm speed-reading, giggling like a five-year-old following the bizarre antics and fatalistic journeying of good old Arthur Dent and Ford Prefect. Nathan always seems to know just what to do to amuse me, to keep me entertained, interested. Without doubt he's the best company I've ever had. Ever.

"Get that gorgeous arse over here. Dinner is served, madame."

I turn, startled. I hadn't been aware of him setting the table or serving out the food, but there it is. Two plates of juicy steak and chips and a bowl of crisp leafy salad, set out on the dining table, plates flanked by cutlery and tall wine glasses. A bottle of red is opened, breathing on the table. Nathan is standing, watching me, holding out my chair.

Self-conscious again but deliberately choking that back, I hop down from my stool and walk towards him, as gracefully as I can, then sit on the chair. He whips a serviette from over his arm and makes a great show of settling it on my lap, positioning it just so and finding it necessary in the process to stroke my breasts and slide his fingers between my legs. Needless to say, I'm wet. He straightens, licking his fingers, one at a time. Christ!

"Mmm, beats a prawn cocktail starter. Help yourself to salad."

While I try to reel in my eyes, which must be out on stalks, he casually sits down opposite me, and pushes the salad bowl in my direction. I grab a few chunks of lettuce and some red stuff—peppers? Tomatoes? I'm too distracted to notice—and plonk them on my plate. The steak looks delicious, smells the same way too. Who'd have thought the luscious Nathan Darke could cook on top of all his other talents?

"Why thank you, Miss Byrne." *What? Did I say that out loud. Again? Must be losing it.* "Comes with the territory—being a father. Can't feed a growing girl on McDonalds and pizza, well, not all the time, so I had to learn to cook decent food occasionally."

"Doesn't Mrs Richardson handle all that?"

"Mostly, yes. But she's an employee so she has time off. Or holidays. So I need to be able to cook, plait hair, dress dollies, read bedtime stories. Would you like me to plait your hair, Miss Byrne?"

I stare at him dumbly, getting my head around this unnerving picture of domestic capability.

"A bedtime story, perhaps?" His head is tilted quizzically, a teasing smile quirking his lips. "No? Well, eat up then, while it's hot." He picks up his knife and fork and gestures to mine. I pick up the tools and start eating.

It's absolutely fabulous. Juicy steak falling apart under the sharp knife, crispy chunky chips, soft and fluffy on the inside, and the salad crunchy and sweet. I munch the first few mouthfuls in silence, savouring one of the best meals I have ever had. After a few more bites I feel I really must comment.

"God this is wonderful. Where did you learn to cook? And when did you do the shopping for all this?"

"I like to cook. I've always been able to rustle up a meal. Maybe it's a bit like you and learning languages, sort of a knack."

I can relate to that. I nod and carry on stuffing my face.

"As for the shopping, I keep steaks in the freezer, and plenty of good red wine to hand. I phoned down to Tesco Express while you were fussing with your extensive wardrobe for this evening and got one of the assistants down there to run up here with a bag of salad and some spuds. Simple."

I make sure my 'extensive wardrobe' is safely tucked behind my serviette — don't want to dangle in the steak juices — and return to the matter under discussion. "They do deliveries? Tesco Express?"

"Of course, if you ask nicely and tip them well. More wine, Miss Byrne?"

"Yes, please." Amazing. From then on I devote myself to the meal, giving it my undivided attention until a few minutes later my plate is clean. I lean back, dabbing my lips as daintily as I can with my serviette. Nathan stands, picks up my empty plate and cutlery as well as his own and takes them to the sink and drops them in. "Can I interest you in a little dessert, Miss Byrne?"

"Mmm, yes, I expect so. What do you have?"

"You'll have to guess, Miss Byrne. But I should tell you, even though I don't have much of a sweet tooth, desserts are a speciality of mine." Then he's behind me, his hands at my neck, loosening my tie. He removes it and quickly repositions it across my eyes, before tying it behind my head.

"Comfortable?"

I nod, expectantly, my hands in my lap.

"Good. Put your hands behind you, please, I'm going to tie you up."

"What? Why? I'm up for this, whatever it is. I'm not going anywhere."

"Your hands, Miss Byrne." His voice has taken that familiar, hard edge. The tone I have come to love, and fear a little. But mostly love. I drop my hands to my sides and he takes my wrists in each of his hands, pulling them behind my back where he quickly ties them together. Leaning past me he takes the serviette from my lap and I feel my chair turn as he pulls me away from the table. I hear the slight scrape of him moving another chair, I assume to seat himself directly in front of me. Tentatively I reach out with my foot, and sure enough, I find the soft denim of his jeans about a foot away from me.

"Wondering where I am, Miss Byrne? Don't worry, I'm right here." He takes my face between his hands and tilts it upwards, placing his lips over mine. The kiss is soft at first, gentle, tentative, then he slants his head to deepen it, sliding his tongue deep into my mouth. I open my lips for him, inviting him in, tangling my tongue with his, letting him suck my tongue into his mouth and nip it gently between his teeth. His hands are firm, holding my face in place, allowing me no choice but to let him have my mouth. He continues to kiss me, deeply, intensely, his fingers tunnelling under the blindfold to tangle in my hair, forcing my head back. I feel the familiar tug of sensual awareness building as he ignites my senses, relentlessly driving my arousal, building that knot of greedy lust I have become accustomed to now.

Then suddenly he lifts his head, releases me, and he is gone. I gasp, moan in disappointment, frustration, wildly waving my head from side to side, blindly seeking him through the blackness of the silk covering my eyes.

He is silent. The room is silent. No clues. I could be alone, but I know better. I can sense him, somewhere near, and the not knowing scares me. My naked, helpless vulnerability scares me. The seconds tick by, then the minutes. I can't bear it.

"Where are you? Nathan, please..." I can hear the catch in my voice, the slight waver that lets him know he has me, that I'm unravelling. Still he is silent. More minutes tick by. Has he left me? Surely he can't have...

"Open your mouth, Miss Byrne."

The voice comes from right in front of me, and I jump to attention. He must be able to hear my heart pounding. Certainly I can. As if he can hear my thoughts he places his hand, warm and soft, at my left breast, flattened to feel my heart thumping under my skin.

"You seem nervous, Miss Byrne. That's good. Now, do as you're told. Open your mouth."

I do, and am rewarded with the delicious sensation of a creamy, sweet mousse dropped onto my tongue. The flavour is fruity and tart, the consistency fluffy. I savour the light, crisp taste, then swallow it, licking my lips.

"More, Miss Byrne?"

"Mmm, yes, please. What is it?"

"Mrs Richardson's special strawberry mousse. A particular favourite of mine. And yours too, perhaps? Open wide…"

I open my mouth to receive another delicious spoonful of Mrs Richardson's culinary masterpiece, and sigh as the delicious concoction slides down my throat. Christ, that woman knows her way around a pudding bowl. Wonderful. Bliss on a stick, or should that be a spoon?

"More?" I nod, and open my mouth. Nathan obligingly delivers another mouthwatering spoonful.

"Mind if I have some?" His voice is soft, as he whispers against my ear. In my delight at the heavenly taste dancing across my tongue I hadn't realised he was so close, but I can feel his breath against my neck, and now his fingertips are fluttering down, across my shoulder to my right breast. Lightly, gently, he feathers his fingers across my nipple, then circles more firmly as the little bud hardens and grows under his touch. My breath catches now, my attention snapping back to the sensuality of his caress and the intimacy of this moment. "May I share, Miss Byrne?"

What? Share what? Ah, right, the pudding. "Of course. Yes. But leave some more for me, please." I'm feeling generous but not stupid.

"So kind. But I don't want to lick mine from a spoon. I want to lick it from you. From your nipples. Is that okay, Miss Byrne?"

Christ! Fuck! "Yes."

Yes, please!

He gives a throaty chuckle at my undisguised enthusiasm. A moment later I wince slightly as the chill of the mousse makes contact with my erect nipples, first one, then the other as Nathan carefully, lovingly applies his helping of the dessert to them. The sensation is exquisite, the cool of the dessert and the warmth of his gentle fingertips. Then I gasp and throw back my head as he takes my right nipple into his warm, wet mouth and sucks. Hard. His tongue swirls around, lapping away the sticky mousse. I groan with pleasure as the sensation spikes, sending a bolt of lightning straight to my groin. I feel the wetness between my legs and I shift in the chair, subconsciously trying to create the friction where I need it. Want it.

Nathan lifts his head from my nipple, just gently flicking it with his tongue. "Be patient, Miss Byrne. Keep still. I'll deal with that in a minute." And by way of making me wait he takes my left nipple into his mouth, holding it lightly between his teeth as he licks the mousse off. The sensation, and the anticipation of what is to come — *please, God!* — is overwhelming. I am writhing in my chair, nearly mindless with desire and desperate for some serious attention between my legs. At last Nathan relents, and effortlessly picks me up from my chair and deposits me on the table. He slides me along the surface until my shoulders are flat on the table top, my hands still bound underneath me, my legs bent and my heels on the edge of the polished wooden surface.

"Open wide, Miss Byrne." I don't need telling twice and I don't even pretend not to get his meaning. I spread my thighs for him and scream with pleasure as he smears a generous serving of strawberry mousse all over my clitoris, and the lips of my vagina. Pushing my knee upwards with one hand he raises me slightly so he can even spread the stuff around my anus. I forget to breathe. With no further ado, using both hands now to cup my bottom he lifts me, legs spread wide, and takes a long, slow lick from my anus right up around my vagina and across my clitoris. I scream again, to be rewarded by sweet, intense little nibbles around my clitoris.

My climax punches forward. I am beyond coherent thought, thrusting under his mouth, greedy and grasping for the delight he is offering me. He holds me still, steady, as he continues to lick every part of me and I unravel in his hands. The orgasm starts right there and seems to go on for hours. I hear myself gasping, then screaming again as the sensation spikes and grips me, as he draws every last shiver of sensation from me. Eventually I'm spent and he lowers me back to the table top, allowing me to lie still, my legs still spread wide, and I'm purring with delight.

Thinking it's all over I start to stretch, only to be picked up again, still bound and blindfolded, and carried across the room. I think we're headed back to bed, but no. He kneels down with me in his arms and places me on the floor. I feel a deep, fluffy rug under me and realise we must be in front of the tinted picture window. Before I can mutter anything along the lines of 'Peeping Toms' and 'draw the curtains' Nathan pushes me around onto my knees.

"Time for seconds. Turn over, please." He sees that I'm struggling to shift, my arms still tied and the blindfold confusing me, so he gently helps me into place. "Lean forward. Put your face into the rug. And open your legs. Wide."

All thoughts of decency and privacy dissipate as he pushes my shoulders forward and I find myself assuming the position. This time he spreads the mousse generously around my bum, letting his fingertip slip inside to tease me and make sure I'm paying attention. I am. Definitely. He slides his fingers between the lips of my vagina to spread the mousse there too, and gently finishes the trail at my clitoris.

"You are one seriously lovely woman, Miss Byrne." His voice is thick with his own desire, seductive, breathy. I feel a zing of pleasure that he seems to want me as much as I want him, if that's possible. His tongue and lips are gentler now, swirling around my anus to remove every last smear before working forwards around my vagina. His tongue dips inside and I gasp, thrusting back against him to deepen the contact. Sensitive as ever Nathan takes the hint, and obligingly tongue-fucks me until I start to come again. Then, before I can get too carried away, he slips his tongue back to my anus, at the same time taking my quivering clit between his finger and thumb. He rubs, licks, and I come apart.

Even before I stop convulsing he is inside me, his thick, hard penis stretching me impossibly. The sensation of fullness is incredible, wonderful, overwhelming. I cry out with the sheer joy and intensity of it. I feel his fingers deftly unfastening the knots at my wrists and my hands are free. He slips the blindfold up and away, and I blink at the sudden light. One hand on the rug to take his weight and the other caressing my breasts, my hips, my bottom, he leans over me. He is sliding in and out, slowly, deeply, achingly gentle. I stretch my arms out, clutching the deep pile rug in front of me, and circle my hips against him. This feels so good, so damn good.

"Do you like it like this, Angel? Long and slow and easy?" His voice is a soft, seductive whisper, a breath against my ear.

I answer him, "Yes, oh God, yes. Don't stop. Don't ever stop."

"I aim to please you, Angel. Enjoy." He nudges my hair aside to nip my earlobe, easing back almost to the point of slipping out of me. He hovers there at my entrance, waiting for me to whimper my need before sliding back in, right to the hilt. He angles his penetration to hit just that spot, deep inside me where he knows the nerve endings bunch, and I stiffen as the warm waves of delicious pleasure wash over me, and through me. Even when I would have started to thrust back against him to force the pace, he holds me, gentle and firm, drawing out the pleasure. He uses his fingers, strumming them continuously across my clit, tickling and teasing and heightening every sensation, but not enough to send me over the brink. Not yet. His gentle, slow strokes build slowly. Too slowly, nudging me towards orgasm again. I am gasping, my breathing heavy, desperate for more. For more, what?

At last I can bear it no longer. "Please, oh God, Nathan, please. I need... I need..."

"This? Is this what you need, Angel?" He strokes my clit more firmly and I arch my back, quivering as he stills to rub my most sensitive spot before withdrawing and plunging back into me, deep and hard. I scream and convulse around him, gyrating my hips to wring every last greedy scrape of friction from his cock as my orgasm ripples through me. With a muffled, "Fuck, ah, my sweet Angel", he thrusts, hard and sharp, and his own climax is here. I feel the hot spurt inside me as his hands grip my hips, holding me in place for his final deep and none too gentle penetration. It feels fabulous as we come together, spiralling away over the edge.

Afterwards we are both lying on the rug, on our sides, my back snuggled against his chest, his arm around me and my bum tucked up against his groin. I can still feel his cock against my buttocks, still semi-hard as his breathing, and mine, returns to normal. We are silent, each of us savouring the moment, enjoying the satiated aftermath of shit-hot sex. Well, it seemed shit-hot to me.

"Nathan?"

"Mmm, what?"

"That was good. That was so good."

"Yes, I thought so too. And like I said, we aim to please, to provide full and complete satisfaction. I'm so glad you approve of my efforts." He pulls me closer, kissing my hair.

"I do. I really do. So much. You've taught me, shown me, so much. And I want to satisfy you too. Completely. I want to make some efforts of my own."

"Do I look to you like a guy who's not entirely satisfied, Miss Byrne? What sort of 'efforts' do you have in mind to top what we just did?"

"What *you* just did. I'm a passenger, along for the ride."

His snort into my hair tells me what he thinks of that. "Mind-blowing sex is hardly a solo performance, Miss Byrne. It takes two to tango and all that. And even you, Eva, the wonder kid, brilliant musician, linguist and mathematician that you are, and a sexy little hot bird into the bargain, would find it kind of hard to be the sexual aggressor when your hands are tied behind your back and you're blindfolded. Your role is — was — to respond. Which you did beautifully, I should add. Passenger my arse!" To emphasise his point he nips my shoulder hard enough to make me yelp, then licks the spot, holding me still as I start to wriggle.

"Keep still while I bite you, that's a good little sub." His voice is playful as he trails his hands lightly over my body, using his teeth to scrape the point of my shoulder, my neck, my ear, his stubble scratching my skin.

"But that's just the point, I've not been—a good little sub, that is. I fainted, duh." Turning in his arms I take his face between my hands, gazing into his eyes. He shakes his head slowly, obviously puzzled, wondering what's eating me now—the creases between his eyebrows deepening as his lips quirk up at one side.

"Are you still on about that? It doesn't matter, love. Really it doesn't. What's one little caning malfunction between friends?"

"But it does matter. And it was a big malfunction, you were furious with me over it. It was part of the deal, the arrangement. Your sheet of dos and don'ts. It was a do." I am staring at him earnestly. I need to make him understand, I mean to prove myself.

"I want to do it again. Now."

"Now? Have a heart, love. Give me a few more minutes to recover then I'm willing to try if you really insist…"

"Not that, idiot." I punch his shoulder. "Caning. I want you to cane me again, and this time I'll do it. All of it. I'll be able to see it through now, I know I will."

Rolling forward he pushes me onto my back and leans over me, his weight across my chest pinning me down. This time it is him holding my gaze, his hands tangled in my hair. His eyes are no longer laughing, his expression is serious, intense. "I know what you meant, and you don't have to do that. Ever. You never need to do that again, love. You've nothing to prove."

"But I..."

"No, listen to me, Angel. I was angry when you fainted, that's true. But not because I had to stop, not because I wasn't finished having my fun with you when you passed out. I was angry because of the danger you put yourself in by not safe wording when it got too much for you. You scared me, really scared me. I thought I'd really hurt you. And I never, ever want to feel scared like that again. I don't want to hurt you. Ever."

"You've never hurt me, and you won't. Not really. I know that now, and that's why I can do it. I know I can. Please, you have to let me try again. I need to try again. I want to be... I want to be everything you want. Everything you need. Please, let me..."

For a long, slow moment he looks down at me, into my eyes, and I hold my breath. Waiting. Silently I mouth the word 'please' again. He starts to shake his head, but my expression must have stopped him from turning me down. Slowly he lowers his forehead to mine. Then he gently kisses me before whispering, "Okay, we'll try again."

"Now?"

"No, not now. Tomorrow, if you still want to. And I hope you don't want to in the cold light of morning. And just so's we're absolutely clear, I've had more sex in the last few days than I've had for months. Mind-blowing, brilliant sex, the sort of sex I've only dreamt about. You are all my fantasies rolled up into one sexy little package, Eva. You absolutely delight me, in every way. You've done all I've asked, and more. I know you've been scared at times, embarrassed. I've outraged your modesty, taken your virginity in every which way I could think of and you've let me. You've responded to me, given me everything I wanted, given me pleasure by sharing your own. You may not be the perfect sub, but who gives a fuck? I don't want just that from you anymore. By now you must realise you're so much more than a sub to me. You're in my home, my family, my life. You absolutely owe me nothing, Eva. You're perfect being just you."

I can only stare at him, wide-eyed, as the words sink in. The wonderful, affirming, empowering words, words that say I'm okay, that I'm perfect even. Maybe. Definitely? Me. And he means it, he really does seem to mean it. My lips are moving, but I have no words to respond. Nathan solves the problem by dropping his head and kissing me, lightly at first then deeply. He slides his tongue between my lips, stroking inside my mouth. His arms are around me and he is holding me, tightly, crushed against his chest, still pinned under him. Uncaring of the weight pressing down on me, my hands tangle in his hair as I return the kiss, desperately seeking to communicate this rush of feeling, this sense of belonging that is so new to me, so alien, and so wondrous.

Eventually he breaks the kiss, lifts his head. I open my eyes to find his gaze fixed on me holding my eyes with his own. "Is that absolutely clear, sweetheart?"

"Is what clear?" I whisper, uncertain.

"How I feel about you, about us, about what you need to do, or not do, to make me happy?"

"Yes. Thank you. Yes."

"No need to thank me, love. It's my absolute pleasure." Then, in one of his trademark mercurial swings, he's shooting off at a complete tangent, "Now, do you feel like going out? On another date? With me?"

Chapter Seven

"Out? You want to go out? At this time?" I realise as I'm saying it that I have no idea what time it actually is, but I feel sure it must be late. A belated glance at the window suggests not—it's not quite dark yet. Nathan, who incredibly has managed to still be wearing his jeans, more or less, digs into his pocket and pulls out his phone. After handing it to me he sits up as I fiddle with the phone to switch it on and get a time check. Twenty-one twelve. Not even quarter past nine. The night is indeed still young...

"Where do you have in mind? We missed the theatre."

"Mmm, pity that. Tennessee Williams will have to keep for another time. That leaves clubbing...?"

I am shaking my head. I don't mind loud, thumpy music occasionally, but I have to be in the mood. And today I'm not.

"No? Fine, what about the cinema?"

I shrug, non-committal. "I'd just as soon snuggle up here in front of a DVD. And we just ate your lovely steak and Mrs Richardson's even lovelier pudding, so a late supper might be a bit of an anticlimax."

"Definitely don't want an anticlimax, Miss Byrne. What about the casino then?"

Now he's talking. I love casinos. I perk up immediately. "That sounds good. But we'd need to get dressed."

"Yes, and a more traditional approach to black tie may be appropriate, I think. Going by that mountain of boxes and bags piled up in my spare room you must have another new outfit needing an airing."

I nod enthusiastically, thinking of the classy little black slinky thing I picked up at Harvey Nicks. I wasn't at all sure where or when I'd get to wear it when I was handing over my credit card, only to be informed that Nathan had everything covered, but it's perfect for this.

Scrambling to my feet I'm itching to get going. "I need to get a shower, wash off what's left of this sticky stuff—you're a sloppy eater, Mr Darke. And I'll need to do something with my hair. Give me half an hour..." I'm halfway across the floor headed for the spare room before his voice stops me.

"Grab your stuff and take it into my room, then use my shower."

"What? Yours? Don't you need to use that? I'm okay with the spare one."

"I don't want you, or your stuff, in the spare room anymore. Share mine. My shower, my room, my apartment. Move your stuff in. Share. Please."

His shy smile, his uncertainty, is what breaks the dam, and happiness just bubbles up inside me. On impulse I run back to him. He gets to his feet just in time as I throw my arms around his neck. His arms come around me and I'm lifted off my feet as he swings me round. I wrap my legs around his waist and grab his face between my hands. I plant a huge kiss on his mouth before leaning back to look into his somewhat startled eyes. "I'd love to share with you, Mr Darke. I warn you, though, I'm messy."

"Yeah, so I heard. A car crash. Still, we'll manage I expect. Now, you head for the shower and I'll move your stuff, okay?"

A quick peck on his lips again, and a pat on my bum, which is Nathan trying to show who's boss, and I'm headed for the shower, this time in his—our— room. I realise I have absolutely no idea now where this relationship is headed or what Nathan wants long term, but I'm living for the moment. And we'll see what it brings.

* * * *

"You look gorgeous."

I'm perched on a padded stool in front of Nathan's dressing table, my mascara and lip gloss scattered among his cuff-links and aftershave. Very domestic. Very intimate. His stuff and mine just blending, mingling, to become ours. I glance up, making eye contact with his reflection in the mirror, ultra smart in his evening wear. I'm happy, content, and I smile as much as I can while painting on lip gloss.

Despite the civilised veneer, he's in a dirty, sexy mood apparently. "I'm just going to smear all that so you're wasting your time." His runs his fingers through my hair, lifting the smooth amber and copper waves, artfully cut, courtesy of Damien, to kiss my neck. It tickles so I shiver—our gazes lock in the mirror. "Why did I have to suggest we go out? Why didn't I just leave well alone and keep you here, with me, all night. I still could. I want you again. Now."

I'm caught between the rush of wetness already forming between my legs—God, I hope I don't stain my lovely new dress—and disappointment that we may not make it for our night out after all.

He sees, relents. "Oh well, I suppose you'll keep. For a couple of hours anyway. But any longer than that and I swear my balls are gonna explode. So, you've been warned, Miss Byrne. You'll be very thoroughly fucked as soon as we get back. It'll be hard and fast, and you'll just have to try to keep up. Okay?"

I nod, dumbly, my lip gloss forgotten. I'm getting used to his crude directness a bit, but it still shocks me. No one else I know—have ever known as far as I can remember—speaks like that around me, about sex and fucking and body parts and, well, everything. And no one has ever made my nipples stand to attention and my pants wet just by making a few crude suggestions. But Nathan can. Does. All the time. It's wonderful.

After shrugging into his own jacket, he picks up mine from the bed, a loose floaty affair in pearl grey that I thought would go with anything. My dress is a black silk sheath, mid-thigh-length and drapes in soft folds around my body. The back is low, the front decent but fragile-looking, as though the folds could drop away at any moments to expose my breasts. It's actually a lot tougher than it looks. Nathan tested it thoroughly earlier, when I first modelled it for him, finally finding his way in by sheer determination and sucking my nipples until I stopped wriggling. He declared a distinct preference for strawberry mousse flavour so I just hope there's plenty more in the freezer. And now, at last, we're ready to go.

The casino is nearby, about a five-minute walk along the side of the dock. Well, ten minutes in my favourite fuck-me red heels, but we're in no hurry. This is a very handy place to live, I'm finding. Who needs a car or taxis? Theatres, the opera, ballet, shops—everything I like within about twenty minutes on foot. Except the moors, of course, but Black Combe and the Brontë countryside seems like another life just now. And while on the subject of other lives, I'm turning over in my mind whether to tell Nathan about my previous experience with casinos…

Maybe I should tell him that I am a fairly regular gambler. Well, very regular. Frequent, in fact. A frequent visitor to casinos, that is. The truth is I'm not much of a gambler, strictly speaking, as it's not really a gamble for me. I invariably win. I take a deep breath. Best get it over with…

"Do you come here often?"

"My, my, what a traditional pick-up line, Miss Byrne. But I'd have thought we were past all that now."

I dig him in the ribs. "No, idiot. I mean do you come to this casino often?" I can see now that we're close that the casino is one of the Alea chain. I have an account with this lot so I probably do need to come clean before we get there. There's a good chance I might be recognised—they rotate the staff around different sites and my face is quite well known in these circles.

"No, not often. I've been a couple of times—they offer special introductory packages for locals to try to drum up regular trade. I've popped in, I like an occasional flutter, but I can manage to lose my money perfectly well through my business in this bloody recession. I don't need to gamble it away as well.

Don't worry, though, I don't mind blowing a couple of hundred quid on a good night out."

"Well, that's just it. You won't be blowing it, probably. Well, I won't. I'll win."

He gives my shoulders a quick hug. "Maybe once or twice. But eventually everyone loses. That's how these places stay in business."

I stop, turn to face him. "Not everyone. I don't lose. Well, hardly ever."

His head is cocked to one side as he considers this. By now he's learnt not to underestimate me apparently. "Eva? Is there something you've not told me?"

"Nothing bad, honestly." I pull my light jacket around me. He might disapprove of professional gamblers for all I know. Although I don't usually think of myself as a professional, exactly, it's just that this is an easy way to make ready cash and I'm not above using my talents when I need to.

"It's, well, it's not unusual, quite common really… For people like me… For…"

"Eva, just spit it out."

I take a deep breath and do just that. "I'm a mathematician. That means I can do a lot more with numbers than just adding up. I can see number patterns, remember sequences, calculate probabilities. So I don't need to gamble, I can work out the probabilities of what card's coming up, where the little ball will land, and only bet when the chances are I'll win. And I do win. Most of the time. I like roulette best. American roulette…" I stop babbling, and fix my gaze on my feet, waiting for his reaction. After all my previous revelations this seems like a small thing to me, but you never can tell.

I wait a few seconds, staring at my red shoes and his shiny black ones, until his finger under my chin pushes my face up again. His dark chocolate eyes hold mine and I cringe, my mouth twisting into an embarrassed grimace.

"So what is it, some sort of system you have? Is it legal?"

"Legal? God, yes! I'm not a cheat. I just… I just follow the sequence of events and predict what's coming next. Anyone can do it, given enough time. I just do it fast."

"No matter how fast you are, how can you predict where the ball's going to land? How can anyone? It's a random event. Poker, yes, you can play that and use your skill to win. Up to a point. But a game of chance? Roulette? How can you be sure of winning at that?"

"It's not random."

He shoots me a look of disbelief and I start to get irritated. How many times do I have to tell him before he believes me? How much proof does he need before he'll accept that I can do what I say I can do? Christ, why lie? It's easy enough to demonstrate after all.

"I'm not going into the detail here, but just believe me when I tell you that particle physics has proven that the universe is not a random system. There is always order, always a sequence to be found. If the sample is large enough, the sequence repeats. Eventually. Otherwise the world would be a chaotic place, which it isn't. Usually. Haven't you ever wondered why it is that time moves forwards, not backwards?"

One glance at his face, his expression of utter incredulity, is sufficient to convince me that this is not a question that has troubled Nathan Darke over the years. I shrug. "Oh well, it must be just me then.

Believe me, though, when I tell you that very little of what happens is ever random. And that's all I do. I watch, wait until I see the sequence of colours, numbers, whatever, until I see the pattern emerging. And then I can forecast what's coming. If I get it wrong occasionally I adjust my perception of the sequence slightly, just to make it more perfect, and go again. I rarely lose. In fact, I can't remember when I last lost."

Those incredulous eyebrows slowly lower as he considers my explanation. And, amazingly, accepts it. Hands on hips, he lowers his head, shakes it slowly before spearing me with his gaze again. "Bloody hell. So you're going to make us our fortune in there, are you?"

I stiffen, straighten. I need to take charge of this, if he'll let me. "No. They'll throw us out if they think we're cheating, if it's too obvious. And anyway, they know me at Alea's and I have a sort of agreement with them. I always limit my winnings to around a couple of thousand pounds."

"An agreement?"

"Yes. I started going to casinos as soon as I turned eighteen, although I'd known since school that I could win at so-called games of chance by working out the number sequences—lots of us could. But I got carried away at first. I was too greedy, and got thrown out of the first couple of houses I tried it in. Then another time a pair of security guards marched me off to the manager's office where I was searched for magnetic devices and such like. God, that was awful. I was so scared, I thought they were going to beat me up and throw me out in a back alley. But once she'd convinced herself I wasn't cheating, the manager was actually very nice. She told me I could carry on gambling in her casino as long as I kept it moderate, as long as I didn't take too much of their cash. Having a winner at the table encourages everyone else to have a go so the house sort of recoups its losses. In a way, I'm good for business."

"But even keeping it moderate, as you put it, you could make a fortune by going around different places, taking just a thousand or two each time."

"Yeah, but I only do it for fun, not for a living. It's how I lay my hands on a bit of spare cash for luxuries, things like foreign travel. I get a lot of time off in the summer and I like to travel, and this is how I pay for it. Or if I want to buy something special—like my violin, for example—I nip into a casino and win the money."

"Like the rest of us get cash from a cash machine?"

"Well, I never thought of it quite like that, but yes. Maybe. It really is quite legal. And doesn't harm anyone. You don't mind, do you? I should have told you all this before we came out. I'll understand if you don't want to go in with me now. We can just go back to your apartment and… Well, you know…"

"Yes I do know. And tempting as the prospect of fucking you is, like I said earlier, you'll keep. Now, I just want to see you in action, in there." He jerks his head to indicate the brightly lit casino entrance behind us, the revolving front door swishing around slowly. "But only on condition you let me buy the chips. It's my treat, after all, I invited you out."

I smile, delighted to have company on one of my gaming excursions. We glide through the doors, nodding to the smartly tuxedoed doorman as we make a beeline for the cashier's desk to get some chips.

Three hours later, around one thirty in the morning we are strolling back around the more or less deserted dock, three thousand pounds richer. Nathan's jacket is loosely hanging from my shoulders to ward off the slight late evening chill, and his arm is around my waist, holding me by his side.

Nathan insisted on buying, and he changed five hundred pounds for chips, which he shared equally with me. He lost his slice of the money within about half an hour, whilst I was still assessing the play at the American roulette table. Then, when I was ready to start playing, he simply stood beside me whilst I placed my bets. I'd decided to keep it simple by betting only on red or black to give myself a fifty-fifty chance without any additional edge from my peculiar talents. It was easy, ridiculously easy, and my winnings built slowly and steadily over the next hour or so. When I reached three and a half grand I decided to call it a night.

Nathan cashed in the chips then handed the wadge of notes to me. I refused, told him to have his stake back and put the rest towards car repairs. His eyes narrowed, he slipped the money into his inside jacket pocket, after peeling off a couple of twenties that he invested in a bottle of champagne. We drank it at a secluded table on a balcony overlooking the gaming floor. I had a wonderful time watching the gaming tables below, subconsciously tuning in to decipher the complex patterns and sequences, and amusing myself watching the many and various reactions of the players as they won or — more often — lost.

Nathan just amused himself watching me. I didn't care, I was happy, enjoying myself, contented. Eventually, the bottle empty and upended in the wine cooler, by mutual unspoken consent we got up and strolled towards the exit. We both knew where we were headed and why. I was already wet.

* * * *

Now, back at Nathan's building, we stand side by side in the lift, in silence, watching the lit-up numbers change on the display above the door. Nathan lifts his hands to slip the knot loose on his bow tie, leaving it to dangle around his neck. He opens the top two buttons on his dress shirt. The sexual awareness is palpable, the anticipation delicious, our intent absolute and clear.

The lift stops at Nathan's penthouse floor and the doors slide open. We step out, cross the landing without looking at each other, without words, and Nathan unlocks the door. He gestures me to go in first, and I hear the gentle click of the lock behind me as I carefully place his jacket, then mine, over the back of the settee. Before I can turn to him Nathan is at my back, lifting my hair to nibble the nape of my neck. I arch and stretch, waiting for him to peel my dress from my shoulders.

Instead, though, he turns me in his arms. Taking my face between his hands he tilts my chin up and his dark chocolate gaze is warm, hot, as he runs his eyes over every feature. He smiles at me, soft and sensual, before dropping his head to kiss me. He starts at my eyes, my cheeks, my ears, my chin, before finally placing his mouth over mine. He trails the tip of his tongue across the seam of my lips and I part them to let him in. He slips his tongue inside, tasting me, teasing me. I groan, the first sound from either of us since we arrived back, and that's his signal to deepen the kiss. His arms slide around my back, holding me firm against him as he tilts his head to strengthen the seal. I press my hands against his chest, savouring the smooth silk of his expensive shirt before reaching up to loop my arms around his neck and just hang on. Without doubt I'd be on the floor if he wasn't holding me upright.

At last, when I am near enough mindless with lust, he raises his head, looking down into my eyes. He straightens, steps away. Sliding the backs of his knuckles down my jaw and across my collarbone, he fingers the black silk of my dress.

"This is a beautiful dress, Eva. Take it off now." The words are spoken softly, his eyes never leaving mine. My lips parted, unmoving, I gaze back as one dark eyebrow quirks upwards. "Now, Eva." He steps farther away from me to sit back on the settee. He leans back, one ankle crossed over his knee as he watches me, waits for me to obey him. He doesn't speak, he doesn't need to. He just waits.

Slowly, facing him, I reach behind me to lower the zip in the small of my back. I shrug my shoulders to let the straps slip off and down my arms. I'm not wearing a bra so my breasts are bared for him and I can see the appreciation in his eyes. He lets his gaze drift from my face, over my body and back again. He smiles, waits. And I let the dress drop to the floor. I am now standing before him in just a pair of bright crimson pants, black hold-up stockings and my beautiful fuck-me red heels. After a few moments I make to complete the strip show, but he stops me with a quick hand gesture, instead beckoning me to him.

I approach, standing between his legs as he gazes up at me. The undiluted lust in his eyes tells me what he thinks of the floorshow, and my pussy clenches in anticipation of what's to come. No longer shy, no longer embarrassed by my body, I am aware of the power I hold now. Power to entice, to arouse. This man wants me, and I want him. I want him so much it hurts.

I start to sway, but Nathan reaches for me, pulling me into his lap. He kisses me again, quickly, before continuing down to suckle my nipples. I lean back, arching into his mouth and can only moan, pleading for more. He promised me fast and furious, and that's exactly what I want.

As if reading my mind he tips me onto the floor and is immediately on top of me. My back is pressed into the thick carpet and he is tunnelling his hands through my hair as he continues to kiss me senseless. He breaks the kiss for a moment, just long enough to pull off my crimson panties and unzip his trousers, then he positions himself between my legs. With no further ado or fanfare, he puts a hand behind each of my knees, pushing my legs up and wide to open me fully before he plunges inside me.

I scream, and come, clenching hard around his cock. He allows me a few seconds for the ripples of orgasm to flow through me, then any semblance of civilisation deserts him and his thrusts are fast, hard, deep, brutal. And within a few seconds he climaxes too. I hear his muffled curse as his body shudders and he forces my legs higher, wider for his absolute pleasure, his total penetration. I feel the bump of the head of his penis against my cervix and rake my nails down his back. The mingled intensity of pain and pleasure has never been more apt than now, and I cry out as the sensations pulse through me, almost as satisfied by his climax as by my own.

As suddenly as the storm started, it stops. Nathan makes no attempt to withdraw from my body, but he does release my legs. I lie still under him, flat on the floor and vaguely wondering why we're not in bed. But really, I have no complaints. That was superb.

He takes his weight on his elbows to gaze down at me. He drops his forehead to mine then lifts his head again to look at me.

"Did I hurt you?"

"Hurt me? No. Of course not."

"I was rough, didn't give you any time to become ready for me. Are you okay? Really?"

Sliding my hands around his waist I pull him closer to me, if that were possible. I raise my shoulders, reaching to nuzzle his chest, flick his flat nipples with my tongue. I hear him gasp and feel the flinch of reaction. I feel the twitch, the slight jerking deep inside me as his semi-erect penis starts to recover, getting ready to do business again. Lying back down, gyrating my hips and squeezing hard around him to better appreciate the sensation of having him buried to the hilt inside me, I smile back up into his concerned, slightly guilty face. But only slightly guilty, thank heavens.

"I've been ready for hours. You could have had me outside on the pavement. That was…wonderful. Absolutely bloody wonderful. So, please, don't stop now."

His worried face cracks, breaking into a wide, delighted smile. Then his expression changes again to become distinctly lustful, his eyes nearly black with desire. "God, you're so beautiful. I could fuck you all night. And I do believe I probably will."

"Mmm, is that a promise, Mr Darke? In which case, please feel free to start again at your earliest convenience…"

He did. We did. All night.

Chapter Eight

I wake up, stretch, groaning at the unfamiliar aches and stiffness in my limbs. I shiver slightly and burrow back under the duvet, pulling it up around my ears. A slight weight falls across my side and I instinctively snuggle backwards towards it. Nathan's arm tightens around me.

Slowly, languorously, I let myself drift awake. I sigh in contentment and nestle tight up against Nathan's chest. We are both naked, our bodies tangled together. Drained. Exhausted. Spent.

We eventually ended up here in Nathan's bed after trying out just about every other viable surface in every part of the penthouse. Floors, worktops, the table—twice. We made good and creative use of the extremely versatile brown leather settee with its built-in restraints. I confess I had been a little puzzled about those leather straps discreetly hidden within it but I now understand these items of special BDSM-friendly furniture can be obtained from the Internet too—who would have ever thought it?

Nathan's arm tightens and I know he's also awake. His semi-erect penis against my bottom is another signal, and he nuzzles the sensitive skin on the back of my neck as his hands drift upwards to cup my breasts. I allow him free access, loving his touch, the feel of his hands on me, and everything else. I roll onto my back to smile up into his face as he pushes himself up on one elbow to lean over me. He drops a kiss onto my mouth.

"Someone needs to go and get the coffee sorted." His long, bed-tangled hair is loose around his face, his smile wide, his delicious brown eyes warm and seductive.

"Why? What time is it?" Blinking up at him, I can see it's broad daylight. The sun is streaming in through the opened curtains.

He reaches over me to grab his phone from the bedside table. "Ten thirty-nine. I reckon that means we've had about five hours' sleep. So, volunteers for getting coffee?"

"It's your apartment. I wouldn't know where to find anything. And anyway, I make crap coffee." I turn onto my side again, this time facing him, and try to wriggle back under the covers.

"Idle slug. Still, I suppose you do need your beauty sleep… Ouch!" He chuckles and rolls out of bed, rubbing his ribs where I dug my elbow in. Through half-closed lids I watch him pull on his jeans and head for the en suite, before I drift off to sleep again.

* * * *

When I next wake up I feel a lot more like facing the day, or whatever's left of it. Nathan's phone is gone, but the radio alarm tells me it's now turned twelve.

Definitely time to get up, particularly as there's something really important I want to do today. If I can just remember what it is…

Ah yes, caning.

I want Nathan to cane me again today. I know he's not keen, but I need him to do it. I need to do it. For him. And for me. It has to be today because we're leaving later to go back to Black Combe and I've no idea when another opportunity might present itself. So, it's today.

Best get on then.

I sit up in bed and find a cup of lukewarm coffee on the bedside table. I taste it—not too bad. I swig most of it before heading for the en suite. In the shower I lean against the cool tiles, reflecting on all the parts of my body that ache, including some parts I didn't even know I had. Christ, last night was some marathon. It was good, better than good. Absolutely bloody fabulous, in fact. But now I'm paying dearly for my over-enthusiastic athletic performance. I keep forgetting I'm new to all this. I only hope Nathan's feeling the strain too, but somehow I suspect he's fine.

We reprised just about all the activities and positions Nathan has introduced me to in the last three days. Except, I realise, he never even suggested tying me up and there was no 'discipline' of any sort. Just sex, plenty of it, mind-blowing and superbly kinky in places, but still, just sex. No whips and canes, no handcuffs.

Butt plugs, yes. Nipple clamps again, yes. I wince and gently smooth shower cream into my tender nipples as I remember the sharp ecstasy of the hard metal clips squeezing the engorged, sensitive buds. Ouch. And wow!

And what that man did to my arse! Oh my Lord, surely that's not legal. And I can't believe I let him do it. I'm blushing just thinking about it. I knelt on the settee, leaning forward with my bum in the air, legs spread wide, while he worked lubricant into me, first with one finger, then two. Possibly three, I'm not sure. Then he fucked me. There. He rolled me onto my back and pushed my knees up to my chest to lift my bum up. He held me still and rammed his huge cock into me. But not before he asked permission. He held me there, poised and ready, and waited until I said it was okay. I could have said no, and that would have been fine too, but he wanted, needed me to say it. I did. I even said please.

I took all of him, and Nathan is not a small man. Not at all small. It hurt a little at first as he pressed for entry, then I managed to relax my protesting inner muscles and accept him, and from there on it was just wonderful. I lay there under him, his cock inside my anus and my legs wide open. His clever fingers did their magic in my vagina, but most of all on my clitoris. And that lovely little horseshoe-shaped vibrator played its part too. Jesus, I had a good time.

I have absolutely no idea how many orgasms I had in the small hours of this morning, or Nathan had for that matter. No wonder we slept the rest of the morning away, well, I did. And no wonder I'm absolutely starving now. I begin to think fondly about breakfast, or maybe lunch, and apply myself to washing my hair so I can get on with finding some food.

Back in the bedroom, wrapped in one of Nathan's lovely fluffy towels—who does his laundry, I wonder?—I drift around the room, finding my clothes. Nathan brought everything through from the spare room and dumped it all in one of the wardrobes, still in the boxes and bags. I start to sort stuff out, hanging things up, folding and smoothing, and admiring all my lovely new clothes. It still bothers me that Nathan paid for most of it, but I suppose that three grand from last night will go some way towards settling the account.

Time to get some clothes on so I start with lovely underwear, a lacy front-fastening bra and matching pants in delicate lavender. Then I choose my nice black trousers, the ones I wore on Friday, the day we went to the opera, and team them with a loose-fitting cream cotton shirt. Then, unable to delay the moment any longer, barefoot, I pad across the room to kneel in front of the chest at the foot of the bed. I lift the lid to survey Nathan's impressive collection of whips, canes, floggers — you name it, it's in there.

I wonder which one he used on me. He probably showed me it, but I was so rigid with fear at the time I doubt I could have even remembered my own name. I stare into the chest for long minutes, remembering Nathan's assurance that this is not necessary and I'm tempted, really tempted to just slam the lid back down and go for some lunch. Forget all this extreme stuff and enjoy what's on offer now.

I know that won't satisfy me, though, and at the back of my mind is the nagging worry that it won't satisfy Nathan for long either. Sooner or later he's going to want this stuff. He's going to want to take a cane or a whip and tie a naked sub to his bed, or strap her to his special sofa, and I don't want that to be anyone else but me. So I take a deep breath, shove my fears into a corner in my head, and reach in. I sort through the collection. And I make my choice.

I lift out a slender, pliable cane. It has a thin leather strap at one end, and I assume that's the loop to go around the Dom's wrist. It wouldn't do for him to drop his cane before the sub has been thoroughly flogged, would it? Shuddering I test the sting of the supple rod against the palm of my hand, gently at first, then harder. I gasp as the pain bites, and the whistle as the cane swishes through the air before making contact is terrifying. Will I hear that sound before the cane lands on me? Yes. Probably. Jesus!

I stand up, close the lid quietly and make for the door. Time to face him.

Nathan is seated at the dining table, engrossed in his newspaper. I'm still barefoot and light on my feet and he doesn't hear me coming. By way of raising the subject I drop the cane onto the table, on top of his newspaper. He looks at it, then lifts his eyes to mine.

"Morning, gorgeous. Or should I say afternoon." He stands, goes over to the kitchen worktop where the coffee jug is gurgling happily and he pours me a cup. He puts it in front of me on the table before returning to his seat. Nodding in the direction of my carefully selected instrument of torture he looks back at me. "I see we're fancying a little sport later. Can we eat first?"

"Food sounds good. Then sport. Shall I cook something?"

"Do you cook, Eva?"

"Well, a bit. I can try."

"Can you rustle up roast lamb, mint sauce and all the trimmings of a Sunday lunch? With apple crumble and custard for afters?"

At my look of horror he chuckles and stands again, swilling the rest of his coffee down his throat. "Thought not. Right then, I know someone who can.

Get some shoes on, we're going out. And whilst we eat I'm going to try every way I can think of to talk you out of this mad little project of yours. Okay?"

I don't need asking twice where food's concerned, and a roast dinner sounds heavenly. Especially if I'm not cooking it. I slip on my lovely comfy Toms and grab my bag, and within a couple of minutes we're in the lift headed for the ground floor.

"You're not going to talk me round, you know." He needs to understand, I've made up my mind on this.

"Maybe I will. Maybe I'll just refuse to do it."

I grab his arm, suddenly panicking as I see all control, and decision-making power in this matter being jerked away from me. He could just say no and there's really nothing I can do, or say, to make him do it. Except beg. Beg him to use me, beat me, not to leave me for someone else who can deliver what he wants. There are tears in my eyes as I look up at him, and I feel my voice cracking a little. "You promised. I trusted you, because you promised. I believed you…" I am in front of him, clutching both his arms, tightening my fingers around the hard muscles.

His gaze softens, my distress is obvious and he clearly doesn't intend to upset me. His hands frame my chin as he bends his head to look down at me, his expression puzzled. "What promise, love?" His voice is soft, gentle. "What did I promise?"

"Not to force me. You promised I could always choose. And if you just refuse I can't choose. You'll force me to do it your way…"

"I meant I would never force you to do something you didn't want to. That you had only to say no or ask me to stop, and I would. And you don't want to do this, do you? Not really. You hated it last time and now you think you have to endure it again, even though I've told you till I'm sick of hearing myself that you don't. You still think you have to honour some sort of bargain, some agreement between us, but that's not true."

"It *is* true. We *did* have an agreement, it was written on your paper, that list of things you would do to me, and things you wouldn't. Caning was there, on the dos. We have a deal. Had a deal."

"If we did have a deal, as you put it, then you broke it by not safe wording when you should have. That was part of our deal too." I start to stiffen, ready to protest, but he's not to be interrupted. Holding my face still his gaze is steady, unrelenting. "But we've got past it. So now we have a new deal, different terms. And I like our new terms very much. So, please, love, drop this other stuff. Please."

I gaze at him in silence. The lift arrives at the ground floor and I hear the doors glide open behind me, but still we stand there, neither of us wanting to break eye contact but eventually it's me who weakens. Closing my eyes I whisper, "I can't. Please, Nathan. I can't drop it. It's so important to me. I need you to do this with me, for me. I need to see this through."

He mutters something that sounds a lot like 'Shit!', then 'fucking stubborn woman', before his arms are around me and he is holding me tight, my tears once more dampening his shirt front. His hands are on my back, gentling, calming, and he kisses my hair. "Okay, love, don't cry, we'll work something out. Please, don't cry over this."

Nathan shuffles us both out into the empty lobby — thank goodness it's Sunday so none of the normal commercial occupiers and their visitors are here to see me making a fool of myself. He shoves me into the equally deserted ladies' loo and helps himself to some toilet roll from one of the cubicles.

"Here, dry your eyes." I do, and he leans against the hand dryer, watching me as I splash water on my face and generally make myself presentable again.

"I'm sorry about that. I guess I'm a bit emotional about all this... This..." I don't know what it is I'm emotional about really, just that the tears are never far away. "Do I look okay now? Will I do?"

"You'll do fine, Eva. Just fine. Come on, there's a roast shoulder of lamb calling my name out there."

And suddenly we're back to our normal, companionable selves, strolling back through the lobby and out into the fresh air, Nathan's arm casually across my shoulders.

"Where are we going? To a wine bar?" I ask.

"A place I know, called Whitelocks. It's a really ancient old pub right in the middle of Leeds city centre, sort of tucked away behind Marks & Spencer's. They do a wonderful roast dinner. You'll love it."

"A pub?"

"Mmm, but not your usual city centre pub with lager louts and smoking shelters and a ninety-inch screen showing European football – not that I mind football, of course, but there's a time and a place. No, Whitelocks is ye olde worlde traditional pub. I think it was there before Leeds was and the city sort of grew round it, shopping arcades got built and somehow they forgot to demolish Whitelocks to make room. So it stayed, and it's still here. It's really popular with shoppers in the week – you need to book a table or you wait hours – but it tends to be really quiet on Sundays. The cook's called Kath and she lives in the block of council flats across the river from us. I hope you're hungry – Kath doesn't do small portions."

"I'm starving. I think I can measure up to Kath's high standards. Must have used up about twenty thousand calories last night so I need to replenish."

"Yes, I do recall you were very active, very demanding. Have I told you before what a fun date you are?"

Laughing, we cover the few minutes' walk quickly, both of us driven on by growling stomachs. Turning onto one of Leeds' main shopping streets I stop to look at the stuff in Marks & Spencer's window before Nathan drags me on. A few yards farther he suddenly turns and pulls me into a narrow alley, literally behind M & S. I thought he was joking about that but he wasn't. Once through the entrance, the alley widens into a sort of enclosed yard with upturned beer barrels as tables and wooden benches. Some shrubs in pots are dotted around to provide a splash of colour and foliage. Two elderly men sit at one of the barrels nursing half-pints of beer, a small Jack Russell terrier on the ground alongside them, but otherwise the yard is empty. The pub entrance is halfway along the alley, a narrow stone doorway with a very weathered and worn doorstep. This place must be two hundred years old at least.

Nodding and mumbling a greeting towards the two old chaps and their dog, Nathan opens the pub door and stands back for me to go in before him. Inside, the atmosphere is exactly what I'd expected. The bar is solid oak, gleaming with polish and adorned with towelling mats. The bewildering array of pumps offers just about every conceivable sort of real ale, with amazing names like Mud Puppy and Yorkshire Blonde. The pumps offer all sorts of explanations about the wondrous origins of the beer, local hops, home-grown barley, cask matured to produce light ales or thick treacly stouts. Nathan orders a half of something called Three Ridings and I decide to have the same.

There are a few hardy souls like us occupying three or four tables. Probably city dwellers, I guess, out for a roast dinner that they don't have to do the washing up for afterwards. We take our beers over to an empty table near the kitchen and sit down. Within moments a bustling elderly woman in a black dress and starched white lacy apron is there, notepad in hand, asking if we're ready to order. The menu is on a chalkboard over the fireplace, but the only choices seem to be between what sort of roast to go for. That suits us. Nathan chooses the lamb, and I opt for the beef.

Kath's in fine form today, both in the quality of her cooking and her portions. She even comes out to do a round of the tables, checking we're all happy. She obviously knows Nathan, and asks after Rosie and Mrs Richardson. As she trots off to the next table he responds to my raised eyebrow.

"I often bring Rosie here when we come to Leeds. And Kath knew Grace before I shipped her off to look after me in the wilds of Haworth — I think they went to school together somewhere in South Leeds."

"Ah." Satisfied, I go back to the important matter of roast beef, and thirty minutes later I push my plate away, stuffed full. Nathan's also finished, and he's watching me carefully across the table, now littered with our empty plates.

"So, your little project. Still hell-bent on 'proving yourself'?" He makes the little commas in the air with his fingers and I bristle.

"Don't make fun of me. This is serious. It matters to me. A lot."

"Sorry, that was rude. Uncalled for. But—I want you to know you have nothing to prove. Absolutely nothing at all. Do you believe that, Eva?"

"I have something to prove to me."

"Yes, I get that. And that's the only reason I'm going along with this now. If we do it, it's for you, not me. And you can back out any time."

"I know. I won't back out, though." I fiddle with the napkin in my lap, unable to look at him. Unable to face the gentleness and regret I can hear in his voice. I can ignore it if I don't see it head on. Maybe.

"Right, I get that too. So we do this my way, on my terms. Okay?"

At my startled look his voice hardens. "Okay, Eva?"

"I… What does that mean? I want it to be like before. It has to be like before."

"It can't be like before. Before, I beat you senseless and that's so not happening this time. So it will be different. This time it'll be controlled. Well, better controlled than before. And you'll be safe."

"I see. How will you…?"

"Well there's always you and your safe words. Except I can't rely on you to get that right, can I?" I am studying my napkin again so he tips my chin back up with his finger. "Can I?"

"I can try. I know what I did wrong before. I know what to expect now…"

"True, and if you say red I will stop. I'll be delighted to stop. But just in case it slips your mind again, this time I won't tie you up. You won't be restrained and you'll be standing—leaning, or bending over, that's up to you. But you'll be taking your own weight. Then, if your legs give way, if you start to buckle, I'll know. And you can keep your clothes on if you want. They offer no real protection so it won't make any difference to the pain, and I won't be hitting you hard enough to risk breaking the skin, but you might prefer to keep your pants up. Again, your choice."

"But I should be naked, surely. At least, my bottom should be."

"Well, it's true that Doms do tend to prefer their subs to be naked, and vulnerable. And accessible for fucking. But that's not what this is about, is it? But having said that, you do have a gorgeous little arse and I'll never get tired of watching you bend over, so perhaps…"

I glance up to see the wicked smile, and realise he's joking. He picks his moments, but I find myself smiling back.

"Bare bum, I think. For authenticity. And you're not to pull your punches or go easy on me. I want this to be real. I have to know it was the real thing, not a game."

"Well, it's always a game. But you have to let me be the judge of how hard to cane you." I start to protest again, but he's having none of it. "These are my terms, Eva. You're a tiny little thing, very slender, and only about a third of my weight. And this is only the second time you've tried doing this. It won't take much effort to get the desired effect, believe me. I pulled my punches, as you put it, last time. And you fainted. So this time, what about if we start light and I increase the pressure if you're managing okay? Would that suit you?"

I consider for a moment, then nod. He continues, "Twenty strokes is the maximum I'd ever have given you, so assuming you're still on your feet we stop there, no matter what. And I'll stop after every five strokes to check you're okay."

"I… Fine. Twenty strokes. How many did I manage before? I mean…last time, before I—?"

"Before you passed out? Thirteen or fourteen. I checked you at fourteen and you spoke to me, told me you were fine…" He pauses to fix me with a wry look. "But of course I now know that you were either lying through your teeth or delirious because you were out cold at fifteen. So tell me, Eva, that cane you chose. Why did you go for that one?"

"I don't know. It just seemed…"

"Light? Thin? Not too brutal? Were you thinking it might be a soft option, perhaps?"

I shrug. Maybe I did have something like that at the back of my mind.

"It isn't. That particular cane is thin and flexible for a reason. It's designed to deliver a sharp, stinging blow. Very, very painful. Excruciating, I'm told—and Louisa knew what she was on about. Would you like me to choose something else, something less…intense for you?"

I gulp, instinctively clenching my soon-to-be-abused buttocks together, but look him in the eye. The mention of another sub, Louisa, apparently a better sub than me, clinches it. "No, that's the one I chose. And I'd like this to be over so can we go now? Can we go back and…and do it?"

"Okay, if you're ready. And if you won't reconsider?"

"I'm ready. But there is one last thing…" I hesitate, not sure how this last request will be received. "Will you make love to me afterwards?"

His face quirks in surprise. "Of course. Don't I always?"

"Yes, but you usually call it fucking. I want you to make love to me instead. Please."

"Ah, right. A not-so-subtle distinction, but I think I can manage that. On this occasion." He smiles, stands and holds out his hand to me as we make our way across the pub towards the till on the bar.

As we stroll back across the city centre neither of us has anything much to say. The walk back takes longer than it seemed to take to get to Whitelocks—we are in no hurry to arrive home it would appear. Eventually, though, we are in the lift, watching the numbers change. Nathan turns me in his arms and, with his hands loosely clasped behind me, nuzzles my nose with his.

"I have one last request of my own. We'll do this if you really want to. Just this once and then no more. I don't want to hurt you like this to have a good time, and I don't need to. Our sex is wild enough, mind-blowing enough, without that. So if we do this it's not for me, it's for you. I need to know that's clear and understood."

"Thank you." My whispered reply seems to satisfy him and he kisses me lightly before leading me out of the lift and into his apartment.

Nathan unlocks the door, and gestures me inside. The cane is still there, on the dining table along with Nathan's newspaper and two empty coffee cups. Nathan closes the door behind us, then leans back against it, waiting for me to make the first move. This is my show now. Christ!

Walking across to the table I pick up the cane, rolling it slowly in my hands. I move to face Nathan, holding the cane out to him. He comes forward slowly then takes it from me.

"Would you accept a painkiller?"

"Maybe afterwards." I quickly kick off my Toms then undo my trousers, letting them fall to my ankles.

Before I can lose my courage I remove my pretty lavender pants too. Nathan picks up my discarded clothing and places it on the table.

"Do you want to keep this on?" He fingers my cream shirt, and I nod.

"Okay. Do you mind?"

He unbuttons my shirt, nodding his approval at my lovely new bra, then gathers the length of the shirt up in his hands and ties it at the front, under my breasts. "Where would you like to stand?"

"Can I lean on the table?"

"Of course." With a gesture indicating I should get into position, he steps away, and I turn my back to him to face the table. Without further ado I lean forward, folding my elbows on the table top and rest my forehead on them. I hear him step forward to stand behind me, and he gently strokes my bare bottom, first one buttock, then the other.

"Last chance, Eva," he whispers. "Are you sure?"

"Yes, I'm sure, for fuck's sake." I grit my teeth, my jaw clamped shut as I hold my breath. After a few seconds I can't bear the wait any longer. "Just do it. Now. Please."

I hear the shrill whoosh of the cane whistling through the air, then I scream as it lands across my right buttock. The shock and extreme pain buckle my knees and I feel sick. I'm shaking, gasping for air.

"Eva?" Nathan's voice is in my ear. "Do you want me to stop?"

"No, no, *no*. Do it. Just do it and don't stop until it's finished."

"Stand up then." I realise I am on my knees, my forehead now resting against the edge of the table. I struggle to my feet again, and lean over, bracing myself for the next blow.

Nathan might not be doing this willingly, but he's doing it well. His next three strokes are delivered in rapid succession and my screams are echoing around the apartment. The fifth stroke sends me to my knees again. My face is on the carpet and I can hear someone whimpering. I guess that must be me. My bottom feels as though it's on fire—I'm in sheer bloody agony. I can't move, and if I do I just know that wonderful beef dinner is coming back up.

Through my haze of pain I know I'm just a quarter of the way there, though, so I have to get up. I start to push myself up off the floor. Nathan is there, crouching beside me.

"Enough?"

I shake my head, past speaking.

"Christ, Eva, this is killing you. Just stop. Now. Please."

I shake my head again and hold out my hand. "Help me up. Please, help me…"

He does, but won't let me bend over the table again until I've had a drink of cool water from a bottle he thrusts into my hands. Eventually, though, it's time and I bend over, bracing myself for the next attack. Before picking up the cane again Nathan says he needs to check I'm okay to continue and I wince as his gentle fingers stroke my flaming backside. No damage done—yet.

I hear that familiar, terrifying whistle and my bottom explodes into its world of pain again. My screams are fading now, with my strength, but my determination is somehow intact and I manage to lock my knees in place and stay upright. The pain is everywhere, centred on my bottom but every nerve ending in my body is on alert. Everything hurts. There's only me and that fucking cane in the world.

Each blow forces the breath from my lungs and I struggle to draw more in. I really am going to throw up... I just need to...

"Red."

No. No, I didn't mean to say that.

"Red, red, *red*." *Is that my voice? It can't be, I'm dreaming. Hallucinating.*

"Fucking red!" *Nathan?*

I hear a clatter on the table and look up to see the cane sliding along the surface, away from me, away from Nathan. Then he is lifting me, turning me, picking me up carefully so as not to hurt me. I am conscious, confused, but limp in his arms. I close my eyes gratefully, one thought whirling round my head. *Did I safe word?*

When I open my eyes again I am face down on Nathan's bed and he is gently stroking soothing cream into my bottom. It hurts—a lot—and I mumble a protest, but I'm too weak to move away.

"Keep still, sweetheart. Nearly done." A few more gentle strokes and he's finished. Sitting on the bed next to me he pushes my shoulder to roll my top half over. "Sit up if you can and take these." I open my eyes to see his palm outstretched with two white tablets on it. In the other hand he has a glass of water. Painkillers. Good idea. I struggle to sit up enough to take the tablets and gulp them down with the water. Then I flop down onto my face again.

Did I safe word?

I definitely didn't mean to, but I'm so glad it's over. Never, never, never again.

"Too right never again." Nathan has moved round the bed and is now lying alongside me. And I guess I've been thinking out loud again.

"And it was me. Not you. I safe worded." Nathan's tone is low and serious. And somehow flatter than I've ever heard from him before, definitely in his Dom moments.

What? How…? I'm baffled.

"It was killing you. I was killing you. And doing it was killing me. I couldn't continue. I couldn't bear to go on, for my sake not yours. So I safe worded. For me." He is silent for a few moments, then, "If I let you down, Angel, I'm sorry. I thought I could do it, for you, because you wanted it so much. But when it came to it I couldn't carry it through. I'm sorry, Angel."

I don't know what to say. So I say nothing, lie there, wait for the painkillers to kick in, wait for my pain-fuddled brain to kick back in too so I can finally start to make some sense of what's happened. Nathan safe worded? Was that what he'd said? He safe worded because what he was doing, what I was making him do was too painful *for him?* It was hurting *him* more than he could stand so he stopped it? Wow!

The painkillers are working and the pain in my bum has dulled to a mere throb. I manage to struggle onto my side, to face Nathan still stretched out alongside me. He is staring at the ceiling, but turns to me as I place my hand on his chest. His hand comes up to cover mine.

"Are we all right, Angel?"

A simple enough question, but I can only stare at him, dumbly, rifling through my brain for some term of reference for this. Nothing comes to mind. So I settle for the only response that seems appropriate.

"I love you." And I'm beginning to wonder if it's possible, just possible, perhaps, that he might, possibly, love me back. I wait. Now's a good time to tell me if he does. The silence stretches between us, but his eyes are deep, dark, looking into mine. Eventually I can bear it no longer. He clearly has nothing significant he needs to tell me and wishful thinking will get me nowhere. Meanwhile, he made me a promise I intend to call in.

"You said you'd make love to me. Afterwards. It's afterwards now."

His face breaks into a slow, easy smile, sexy and playful, that familiar gleam back in his eyes. "Indeed I did promise you that, Miss Byrne. Are you ready?"

"Oh yes."

He pushes me flat on the bed and leans over to kiss me—long, deep and tender kisses—gently nudging my lips apart with his tongue then darting inside to taste me. The kiss is unhurried, exploring, testing, taking, and I open my mouth to accept. My tongue tangles with his, and he sucks it into his own mouth. I join in the game of dart and thrust, running my tongue along his teeth and trying to pull my tongue back when he nips it lightly. He's not letting go, and we roll together until I'm on top, kissing him. Tunnelling my fingers through his long dark hair, silky and soft, I lift one leg to straddle him. The pain in my backside is still there, but not enough to slow me down now.

While I'm busy kissing him he's busy untying my blouse and sliding it from my body, closely followed by my bra.

Then, satisfied that I am now naked, he rolls again and I am underneath. Now his mouth is moving down, across my chin, my neck, my shoulders, to suckle my nipples. God I love this, and I arch under him in silent approval. He gets the message and the pressure deepens, only slightly, but enough. Then he is going lower, dipping the tip of his tongue in my navel before nibbling downwards, across my sleek, smooth body and between my legs. I open them without any encouragement, wide, welcoming. Needing. His tongue circles, then flicks my clitoris and I gasp, my hands again sinking into his hair to hold him there. He continues to lick my clit, pausing occasionally to graze it with his teeth, and I cry out as the sweet sensation builds and bursts. As my climax starts to subside he gently slides two fingers inside me, angling to press that one spot deep within where all the nerve endings seem to meet and I go off again like a firecracker. He coaxes two more orgasms out of me with his tongue, his teeth and his clever fingers. My limbs feel weightless, boneless, when at last he stands up. He undresses quickly, all the while watching me as I lie there, waiting for him. In seconds he's back.

"This is your show. How would you like this, darling? What's your favourite way?"

"Me on my back, you on top," I whisper.

"Excellent choice, if a little traditional. This okay?" His wonderful cock enters me, gently, slowly, delicately. My arms flung either side of my head, I writhe under him, loving the fullness, the stretching as he sinks fully inside me. My legs curl around his waist, my ankles hooked behind his back. He withdraws smoothly, to slide back in again, and I moan with joy. The feelings are so perfect, so exquisite, and he leans in to kiss me. The kiss is sweet, slow, open-mouthed and sensuous. Whatever he might say, or not say, I have never felt so loved as I do at this moment. His strokes continue, slow, lazy, easy, and my pleasure mounts, growing and curling around my body like smoke. No pain now, no shock or fear, just the delightful, beautiful joy of being filled by a man who cares enough to do this for me. With me. The sweet ecstasy of perfect lovemaking.

My orgasm creeps up slowly, quietly, rolling over and through me as I shudder and squirm under Nathan, my small gasps of pleasure swallowed as he continues to kiss me, as he murmurs wonderful things into my ear. How much he wants me, how gorgeous and sexy I am, how much he needs me. The convulsions fade and with a last deep thrust I feel his semen shoot into me, hot and wet. Afterwards we cling to each other, every part of our bodies touching, and I'm not sure where he ends and I begin.

For now, it's enough.

Chapter Nine

"I guess we need to be heading for home. Black Combe. And Rosie. I wish..." My voice trails away – I'm not entirely certain what it is I wish.

I feel Nathan's arm tighten around me. "There's no hurry, we can stay in bed all day if we want. I'll do my best to keep you amused."

I roll over in bed, snuggling in close to Nathan, my cheek on his chest. I can hear his heart beating – or maybe it's mine. A good sign anyway – at least one of us is still alive. But no matter how long we delay it for, we do need to be making for home sometime soon. And I can hardly bear the thought that our exclusive slice of time together is almost over. It's been weird, an oasis, our own intense little exclusive bubble where we've focused in on each other, oblivious to the outside world. That hostile, demanding, intrusive world of home, family, universities, work, responsibility.

So much has happened – awful and wondrous. I've faced my deepest fears and insecurities and I've touched my dreams. Played out fantasies I hadn't even known I had. It's a work in progress, I'm still a car crash in parts, but I'm getting somewhere. I've discovered new aspects of me, a me I like, a me who has fun. Who *is* fun. A me that will happily roll around naked in bed—and pretty much anywhere else—with a gorgeous and sexy man I've known for only a couple of weeks. I've discovered that there are other possibilities for me, other ways I can be. Will be. There's no going back even if I wanted to and I know I will never feel the same way about myself, about the people around me, about my work, my talents, my future, ever again.

I sigh and roll back over, ready to face reality. Eventually, in a little while. "I'm sure you'll try your best, but you'll appreciate my standards are quite high these days, Mr Darke." Then, more seriously, "I'm looking forward to seeing everyone again, but it's been so wonderful, and I don't want this weekend to be over. And it's just too much trouble to move. When are they expecting us?"

"I'm confident I could find some way to convince you to move. But to answer your question, we're not expected till late. I phoned Grace and told her we've got tickets for the ballet in Bradford. Still want to go?"

Not straight home then. Marvellous.

"Hell, I forgot all about that. *The Nutcracker.* I haven't seen a ballet in ages. Do we still have time?" I start to sit up, suddenly eager, and clutching at the straw of extending our little twosome for a while longer yet. He chuckles at my powers of recuperation.

"Yup, but we need to get moving. Glad rags again, Miss Byrne. Race you to the shower."

* * * *

Hours later it's turned midnight and we are, at last, heading slowly through the pitch black country lanes above Haworth, towards Black Combe. I can't help but remember the last time I made this journey, just me and Miranda in the pouring rain. His usual sensitivity on overdrive, Nathan knows where my thoughts are and with a glance sideways at me he briefly touches my knee.

"It felt like a different journey on your own, I expect. When you were coming up here for the first time."

"Too right. God, I was so nervous. Terrified, in fact. I was lost. And late."

"And I didn't help, crashing into your car and yelling at you, in the rain. You looked like a drowned rat, a little lost waif and I was a total bastard to you."

"Well, I was a bit of a cow myself, I daresay. And your lovely car was all bent."

"My penis substitute…"

"Christ, did I really say that? You should have fired me on the spot."

"I probably would have if I'd realised you worked for me at the time. I was so fucking angry that night and you got the full benefit of it. Crashing my Porsche pissed me off, but I wasn't just pissed off at you. I'd had a really bad day, and then an even worse evening and you got the fallout, both barrels. At first I had you down as some nasty little petty thief looking for pickings at a lonely house. I was intending to rough you up a bit and then hand what was left of you over to the police. When I realised you were a girl I decided just the police would have to do. Still, I've roughed you up a fair bit since…"

"I've survived it. So far."

"Indeed you do seem to have, against all the odds, and I'm very relieved. You've given me some nasty moments." Pausing for a moment to change down through the gears for a particularly sharp bend, he's suddenly back with one of his Mr Mercurial moments. "Are you happy, Eva?"

That was unexpected and I glance across at him. Caught off guard, I blurt out my answer. "Yes. God, yes! I've had a wonderful time, here at Black Combe and with you in Leeds. I've just had the best weekend of my life. And I am glad to be back too. Or I will be."

"Really, Eva? The best weekend ever? All of it, are you sure? The waxing? The caning?"

I pause to think, but not for long. I have absolutely no regrets about any of the things I've done, things I've agreed to. Things I've let him do to me. There isn't anything I wouldn't do again—except the obvious cock-up, but we're past that now. "Yes, all of it. Even those bits. But especially the fucking, as you'd put it. I prefer to think of it as making love, though."

"I didn't have you down as a romantic, Eva."

I decide to ignore him—this is too close to my heart and I feel raw, uncertain of where I stand with him now that our beautiful time together is over. And anyway, I realise, it's not about romance, it's about self-respect.

I continue on as though he never interrupted me. "And I've loved the laughing, the walking through the city centre late at night, the casino, the opera, your guitar, your apartment with the sheep on the roof and your huge bed. All of it. And I love Black Combe too. The house, the moors, these wide open spaces and twisty little roads. So I'm glad to be nearly home. Glad to be seeing Rosie and Mrs Richardson again. And Barney."

"Are you a romantic, Eva? Tell me why you prefer making love to fucking."

So much for my attempt to change the subject. Evidently not happening. And he knows just the right question to ask. He's not letting up, and as ever he's ready to precision bomb my least defended areas. This bombing raid bears some thinking about so I sit in silence for a while, turning over his missile in my head, carefully constructing my answer to it. The minutes pass as we draw closer to home and for once he's patient, waiting, allowing me the time I need to work this through. At last, as we make the turn into the narrow lane leading to the Black Combe gates, I respond.

"I love them both, and I'm not sure where one ends and the other begins always. I love the excitement, the pleasure of hard, rough sex that makes me scream. I like the toys, the erotic games — even the ones that hurt or scare me at first. All of that's fucking, I think. But then there's the holding me while I cry, while you're still inside me. There's the kisses, the sweet words, the kindness and generosity. Sending me a waterproof coat because you think I need one, offering to take me to my father's grave. That's lovemaking. And I can't untangle them. Love and lust, in perfect harmony. That's how it looks to me."

A brief, considering silence, then he continues, "Good answer, Miss Byrne. You did say you were a fast learner. This conversation in *not* done with yet. We'll take it inside." The car glides through the opened gate and comes to a halt on the crunching gravel in front of Black Combe. The house is in darkness as we get out in silence, leaving all my new clothes safely stowed in the boot. We walk around to the back door. Nathan pulls the key from his pocket and lets us in. Apart from the thump thump of Barney's tail hitting the flags as he recognises his nocturnal visitors and Nathan muttering something along the lines of 'some bloody guard dog' as he strokes the huge head, the place is silent. Mrs Richardson and Rosie must be long gone to bed.

Nathan picks up the kettle and with one inquiring eyebrow arched offers me a drink. I nod and sit at the table, idly tugging on Barney's ears while Nathan fixes the drinks. He waggles a packet of Earl Grey teabags at me, and I nod again. A few minutes later he is seated opposite me, both of us clutching a mug and looking at each other across the table.

With a warm smile across his handsome face, Nathan holds out his hand to me. I take it, and for a few moments just concentrate on the smooth play of his thumb across my knuckles. He takes a deep breath, breathes out slowly then starts.

"I've done a lot of fucking. A fuck of a lot over the years. With a lot of different women, a lot of different subs..." His wry smile is mischievous, but I know better than to be fooled. I wait, and his hand tightens around mine. He tugs it towards him and lifts it to his mouth, kisses each of my finger ends before lowering it to the table again. "But very little lovemaking. Pretty much none, actually. Until just recently and I just sort of drifted into it. With you. I care about you and I have absolutely no idea how and why."

Insulted, I stiffen and try to pull away, but he's stronger and not letting go. "Well, maybe I'm starting to have an idea, now that I know you and I've found out what a wonderful, fascinating, exciting, beautiful, intelligent woman you are. You captivate me, Eva. You take my breath away."

I'm staring at him, open-mouthed. This I did not expect.

"I wanted you from the first time I saw you and I tried to make you into my sub because that's what I'm used to. I understand that sort of relationship and it satisfies me. Or always did, till now. But you're a pretty unimpressive submissive, we both know that. And, Eva, please stop looking daggers at me and trying to pull your hand away. You do know how forceful I can get if you challenge me and now's not really the time. You so do not want to be tied up and your nipples clamped when we're having this conversation."

I consciously relax my hand, my arm, and watching him over the rim of my mug I slowly take a sip of my tea. I put the mug down and place my other hand over his. "Go on."

"I want you. It's that simple. I want to fuck you till you scream. And I want to spank you, tie you to my bed, spread your legs and make you come in a million weird and wicked ways. I want to hurt you and then kiss it better. And as long as you never look back on any of it and think, 'I really wish he'd not done that', then I reckon we're okay. But sometimes I want to fuck you slowly, and so gently that it makes you cry, and then I'll hold you until you stop crying. I want to play with you, sleep with you, wake up with you. I want to talk with you, understand you, admire you. I want to care for you. And I want you in every part of my life. Stay with me, Eva. Please."

"You want me to stay? But I thought I was... We'd already..."

"Yes, we have. But I'm not talking about a place to live. I'm talking about you being my..."

I wait, watching the confusion flit across his face as it becomes clear he has no idea at all what he now wants me to become. "Your trainee sub? Violin tutor with benefits?" I offer. I do try to be helpful.

"Do not take the piss, Miss Byrne. I've warned you." There's a familiar glint in his eye as his voice hardens, but I just gaze at him, unfazed.

"I do think you might benefit from some further training, and I would certainly enjoy providing it. But we both know you'll never amount to much of a sub. You're too stroppy, too ready to argue. Too ready to giggle at me, Miss Byrne." His eyebrows lowered, he is trying to give me his very best stern look, but failing. With a wry smile, his head cocked to one side he leans back, watching me closely as he considers his next words. "And it cuts both ways. I'm a rubbish Dom around you. The first whimper of real pain and I'm safe wording like a bloody girl."

"Whimper! I'll have you know I was in agony. That cane was bloody killing me."

"Yeah, and I just couldn't do it. Don't want to do it anymore. I've no stomach for hurting you, Eva, not really hurting you. So it's just kinky fun and games from now on, nice, gentle fucking—but with bells on when we feel the urge. Sound good to you?"

"Bells?"

"Please don't be obtuse, Miss Byrne. It's beneath you. I'm talking about clamping your nipples, about butt plugs and floggers. I'll tie you up, wax you frequently, and you have one hell of a spanking coming your way for all the grief you've just given me while I've been trying to tell you how I feel about you. Ah, I see by your face that you get my drift. But to answer your question, I want you to stay as my...lover. Will that do?"

I think for a moment, just to keep him on his toes, then I'm around the table and climbing into his lap.

My arms around his neck I give my answer, "Yes, yes that will do very well. I'd be delighted to be your lover, Mr Darke." I kiss him, then pull back. "But there's one condition. And it's important. To me. This is a deal-breaker, Mr Darke."

He lowers one worried eyebrow, his mouth flattening. "Go on." His expression is wary, hesitant. Maybe he feels he's conceded enough ground already. Tough.

"I know there've been others. Many other subs before me."

He nods slowly, and I think he's getting my drift so I continue, "But I need to be the only one now. As long as we're...together. No fucking anyone else. Is that agreed?"

To his credit, there is no hesitation in his response. "Yes, Miss Byrne. Agreed. Absolutely. And it cuts both ways. This is exclusive, as long as it lasts. As long as we last."

I'd taken that as read. Hell's bells, I might be a randy little slut these days but only with him. I'm hardly promiscuous. But, for the avoidance of doubt, I agree readily, "Of course. And there's something else I need to say, before we leave this subject."

"Oh. And what's that then, Miss Byrne?" He leans away in order to look me fully in the face, wary once more, anticipating more un-sub-like demands I don't doubt.

"Just that you are absolutely the nicest person I've ever met, ever known."

His expression is one of shock, closely followed by a delighted smile. His next words are perhaps a belated and doomed attempt to re-establish some Dom-like authority.

"Nice? Is that the best you can come up with, Miss Byrne?"

"Nice with bells on then." And, enough said, I go back to kissing him.

* * * *

Later, lying in bed — on my own — I reflected that as declarations of love go, that was up there with the best, even though we both managed to avoid the 'L' word. We held hands as we climbed the stairs and strolled slowly along the landing. Nathan kissed me at my door, and went to his own room. He said he'd explain things to Rosie first chance he got.

Now it's Wednesday, three days later, and he still hasn't found the chance. We've had a lovely few days with Rosie, walking the moors, tenpin bowling, even ice skating, which was an unmitigated disaster as far as I was concerned. My bum still aches, and not in a good way. Me and Rosie have got back into our lessons, and each teatime has seen us playing the violin together to our audience of three. Four one time, when Tom dropped in to bring the quad bike back.

Nathan is a lot of fun as a dad and Rosie adores him. I love watching them together, laughing and cuddling and playing stupid games. Whoever heard of Poohsticks for Christ's sake? With Mrs Richardson and Barney we make a reasonable version of a happy family and I love it. And talking of family I've even started to return my mother's calls, just to assure her that I'm still alive and doing okay. She asks a lot of questions and I'm quite good at being evasive — years of practice, probably. I'm not sure why I don't want her to know I'm shacked up with Nathan Darke in the middle of nowhere, but I just don't. Not yet.

Life at Black Combe is contented, happy and very, very chaste.

I can hardly look at Nathan without wanting to jump him. I can't believe how desperate I am to get laid—our few days in Leeds really whetted my appetite, an appetite I hadn't even known I had. I do now.

There's plenty of touching, kissing and once even a particularly wonderful grope in the garage when he slid his hand into my pants and made me come in about five seconds flat. I offered to suck his cock in return, but he was having none of it. Rosie might come in.

I understand. I do completely understand about being careful around Rosie. But still…

I guess Nathan's just as frustrated as I am because later that day, while we were all enjoying a late breakfast together around the kitchen table Mrs Richardson announced her intention of doing a spot of shopping in Bradford followed by perhaps lunch at Nando's and then a film. She asked for volunteers to keep her company and Rosie spilled her cornflakes as she jumped up and down in delight. I was a little surprised—Grace had said nothing earlier about intending to go out, when we were chatting over coffee. Indeed, I'd had the distinct impression she was planning to spend the day gardening. Still, Nando's is always tempting so I was about to offer to join them myself, but was otherwise engaged grabbing a tea towel to mop up the mess.

Before I had a chance to make any hasty decisions, and as it turned out spoil a seriously good day, Nathan leapt in with plans of his own. He needed to go over to Greystones, he told us, some stuff to talk through with Tom, details for the festival and such like. And would I like to come with him?

Nando's is nice, but the prospect of some 'just us' time with Nathan is much, much nicer. A no-brainer really. I smiled, said I'd love to go to the farm with him.

"I thought we'd walk rather than take the car. That okay with you?" Nathan's smiling at me as we wave Mrs Richardson and Rosie off.

"Yes, lovely." Greystones is only about half an hour's walk away, straight across the moor. It's much quicker on a quad bike, I gather, but that's a skill I've yet to master. Walking's good, though, especially as today is one of the few days this summer when it hasn't rained. I nip off upstairs to find my lovely hiking boots, the ones Nathan gave me as a surprise present soon after I arrived here, and decide to take my waterproof jacket along just in case.

Ten minutes later we're strolling, hand in hand, along a footpath marked with bright yellow acorns, heading uphill onto the moors behind Black Combe. Barney invited himself along with us so he's ambling behind. We pass a couple of other intrepid souls coming in the other direction, Brontë Way enthusiasts no doubt, maybe headed for the *Wuthering Heights* shrine at Top Withens. Everyone's sociable out here on the moors so we nod, murmur our "good days", and carry on. I glance back and see our new friends are taking a somewhat muddy detour from the path, giving Barney a wide berth. He's just standing watching them, bless him, but he is definitely a formidable sight. I take pity and click my tongue for him to stop tormenting the tourists and catch us up.

The landscape is particularly eye-catching today. The late summer wildflowers are glittering, their bright whites, golds and purples contrasting sharply with the lush greens brought about by the copious amount of water that's descended upon us this year. I remember vividly my first encounter with the Oakworth moors — I nearly bloody drowned that night in rain of biblical proportions. I recognise some of the flowers — the purple candle-like flowers of the vervain, and the bright orange snapdragons in the marshy spots. I can also pick out clumps of touch-me-nots hiding in the shade, and the pretty white flowers of the virgin's bower as it clambers and trails its way through the hedgerows.

For all that he's lived here for four years, Nathan seems to not know any of the names of the flowers, although he agrees with me that they're very pretty. But can I please get a move on and stop poking about in the grass! I smile sweetly at him, and poke some more.

Eventually we crest the rise overlooking Greystones, and can see the stone farm buildings below us in the distance. The house is solid, sturdy like Black Combe, though not as big. Three, maybe four bedrooms. I know that the ground floor has a large kitchen, and a spacious lounge with a huge wall-mounted television, site of many laddish football and beer fests in the past, I gather, though Nathan hasn't spent any evenings here since I've been at Black Combe. There's also a dining room, but I get the impression it's not used a great deal as pretty much all activity is centred on the kitchen — if it involves food — or the television.

There's also a huge barn, set at a right angle to the house. The two buildings share a cobbled yard where chickens tend to scratch around and Tom's two border collies try to round them up. Today, though, the dogs are nowhere to be seen, and neither is Tom's Land Rover.

"Looks like he's out. Was he expecting you?" I'd assumed Nathan had arranged to meet Tom here, but apparently not.

Nathan just shrugs. "He'll be around somewhere. We'll wait for him." He catches hold of my hand and tugs me in the direction of the farm.

Ten minutes later we're in the cobbled farmyard being investigated by a crowd of fractious chickens and two extremely belligerent and very noisy geese. I'm much happier poking at wild flowers than cosying up to hostile poultry so I stick close to Nathan. He seems unconcerned, just marches up to the front door and tries the knob. It's locked.

"You're right, he's not here." *Well, duh, no Land Rover, big clue.*

I just nod, thinking it's been a lovely walk anyway, in spite of all the squawking and hissing now coming from the guard-geese.

"Come on, let's have a look round." Again, Nathan grabs my hand and tows me off, this time in the direction of the barn. I follow willingly, anything to put a bit of distance between me and those geese. The massive barn door opens off the courtyard. Originally it would have been designed to accommodate a cart, presumably laden with hay or whatever farmers of yesteryear needed to shift about the place, and is now well big enough for a tractor. Nathan lets go of my hand and shrugs off his waterproof jacket before heaving it open. He leaves his jacket dangling from the oversized handle on the outside of the door and steps inside. I follow him. Barney seems not inclined to join us inside, preferring to plop himself down close to the outer wall, in a patch of shade. The geese, mercifully, seem satisfied that they've successfully defended their territory and driven us out of the courtyard. Barney clearly doesn't count. They quieten down and make no attempt at pursuit.

The barn is huge and dappled with light streaming in through windows high up in the roof. Nathan has moved to the middle of the building and is standing looking up into the loft above his head. I stay where I am by the door, a little awed at the size of this space. Despite its use for animals, and farm storage, the place is remarkably clean. The floor has obviously been recently swept, and the structure is watertight and sound. I suppose Tom Shore would insist on that—he seems the type to want things in good order.

There are no animals in residence just now, unless you count the semi-wild cats slinking around in the loft. I point a couple out to Nathan.

"Yeah, Tom likes to keep cats around. Controls vermin."

I shudder. "Vermin? You mean rats? Are there rats in here?" I'm looking around me wildly now, and I rush to get close to Nathan again. He can fight off any rats. And the geese if it comes to it.

"Can't see any. I expect the cat strategy works pretty well."

I certainly hope so, but I'm not sure I'm totally convinced. Nervous, I try to steer Nathan back towards the door. "Well, there's no one here. Shall we go? We can always come back later, when he's in. Maybe phone him to make sure…?"

He's not going anywhere, apparently. Instead, he turns to me, a familiar gleam in his gorgeous dark eyes. "You're right again, Miss Byrne. He's definitely not here."

Miss Byrne?

He continues, "But we are. Just the two of us. I think we could put this barn to good use. Fancy a little ball game?"

"I… What?" Ball games sound sort of interesting, but the thought of those rats lurking in the corners, hiding, watching me. Waiting…

His tone is slightly mocking as he continues. "You heard. And stop looking so worried — there are no rats here. Or is it me you're scared of?"

I look up at him sharply, surprised he'd even want to ask that. "You? No, of course not! But are you sure? About the rats, I mean?"

"Yes. Certain. Now, about those balls…"

I regard him carefully for a few moments, and cast one last look around the barn. No harm in checking. Then, "What if someone comes in? While I'm doing whatever you have in mind, with your balls?"

"No one's coming in. And I'm not talking about my balls, though you're very welcome to play with them too, if you've a mind to. Later. No, I'm talking about your balls." He grins wickedly, clearly finding my baffled expression amusing. "These balls, to be exact."

He slips his hand into the front pocket of his jeans and pulls out a small cloth sack, the sort you might get from a jeweller's. It's made of red velvety fabric, and closed by a drawstring around the top. He dangles it from his forefinger, swinging it hypnotically in front of me.

"What's that?" I ask suspiciously. "Nipple clamps?"

"I said a ball game, Miss Byrne. You need to concentrate. Though if you want nipple clamps too I could certainly improvise something for you. Would you like that?"

"No. No, thank you. Though it's kind of you to offer." I'm beginning to enter into the spirit of this now, and can feel myself starting to moisten. And I'm desperate to know what's in that little bag. I reach for it, but he whips it behind his back.

"Say please, like a good little sub."

"Please. Sir." I add the last for good measure, though my sarcastic tone is somewhat less than submissive.

He just smiles, shakes his head sadly. "You'll have to do much better than that, Miss Byrne. Say please nicely. And mean it."

His voice has hardened, become firm, unrelenting, and I know this is serious now. This is Nathan in Dom mode, and with some surprises on offer. This means I'm in for a hard time, possibly, but I know it'll be worth it. It always has been. And Nathan the Dom can always bring out Eva the submissive—effortlessly it seems.

"Please, sir, show me what's in the bag." This time my tone is soft, respectful. Suitably subdued. It works, and with a smile he drops the bag into my outstretched palm. I carefully untie the string loop around the top and open it to peer inside.

There are two small, egg-like balls in the bottom of the bag. They look to be held together with a piece of cord. I pour them out onto my hand, and they roll jerkily across my palm before I close it around them. At first I thought they were made of metal because the bag seemed heavy, but now I see they're made of some sort of silicone. The linking cord is silicone too, and has a longer length at one end. As I hold them in my hand I can feel that they're weighted inside to cause the uneven rolling motion. They remind me of some magic beans I once had as a small child—I played with those for hours, marching them down the stairs. I somehow doubt that's what Nathan has in mind now.

But what does he have in mind? I glance up at him questioningly. "What are these? Sir?"

He smiles at my belated politeness. "Very good. But you do need to practise. I want that to roll off your tongue rather better. And talking of rolling, and tongues, though that comes later, these are Ben Wa balls. Or something very similar." At my puzzled expression he continues, clarifying for me. "They go inside you. And the weights in them make them roll and move around when you do. Wonderful sensation. Or so I understand. Would you like to try them, Miss Byrne?"

I tighten my hand around them, rocking it from side to side to feel the shifting weights inside the little egg-shaped balls bumping and rolling against my fingers. It does indeed feel…sensual. And I can only start to imagine how that will feel inside my vagina. But still, here? In a barn? Where Tom or one of his farm workers might walk in on our little floorshow at any time? Where there might even be rats lurking in corners, no matter how efficient the feral cats?

I get no time to ponder further on the wisdom of all this. "If you wouldn't mind, Miss Byrne, I'd like you to undress, please. I want you naked for this."

"Naked? Here?"

"Yes, Miss Byrne. Naked. Here. Now." His tone is stern and unrelenting, and he expects no further debate. I know when to back down, so I take a deep breath, and start to undress.

"I'll take your jacket, if you don't mind. And the balls." He holds out his hand, and I pass him my Rohan jacket. He takes the balls in his other hand, before slipping them into his pocket. As I crouch down to untie the laces on my tough walking shoes and roll off my socks, he strolls over to where several large bales of hay are stacked against the far wall of the barn, directly under one of the roof lights so bathed in summer sunshine. He spreads my jacket across the top of a bale, about three and a half feet high. I guess that's where we're going to be playing, then.

He turns back to me, leans back to prop one hip against the edge of the bale, and watches me while I continue to undress. I'm no longer shy around Nathan, but I am terribly conscious that we could be disturbed at any moment. I don't doubt Tom will have no objection to our being here. He probably won't even mind what we're doing in his barn as there are no animals in here for us to scare. But even so...

I swallow my doubts—no point at all in voicing them when Nathan's in this mood. Best to go with it and enjoy the fun. It only takes me a couple of minutes to lose the rest of my clothing, which I fold and place neatly beside me on the floor of the barn. When I'm finished, I stand back up straight and wait for his instructions. I've learnt it's generally best not to anticipate. Sure enough, he waits for a few moments, clearly enjoying the sight of me naked, surrounded by farm machinery and bales of hay, and ready for whatever he chooses to do next. At last, he beckons me to come over to him. I walk carefully across the floor, conscious that I'm barefoot. I'm still far from happy about the possibility of something fast and furry shooting out from under the hay. And I definitely don't want to step in anything they might leave behind...

When I reach him, Nathan drops a quick kiss on my mouth before placing his hands on my waist and lifting me effortlessly onto the bale of hay behind him. He seats me on top of my jacket, my legs dangling. He places his hands on the inside of my knees and parts my thighs enough that he can stand between them. He rakes my body with his eyes, which if anything seem even darker than usual, then he slips his hands behind me to pull me towards him. He kisses me again, this time a long, deep kiss. His tongue is inside my mouth, and he tastes wonderful. I tangle my hands in his hair, loving the smooth softness of it as it slips between my fingers. Then my tongue is in his mouth, chasing his tongue, tangling with it as he sucks and nibbles. Then he gently scrapes his teeth across my lower lip before drawing that into his mouth. He moves his hands lower, cupping my bottom as he continues to play with my mouth, seemingly in no hurry to move this along. Me neither, as I manage to completely forget all my earlier concerns about unwanted company, of either the two-legged or long-tailed variety.

At last, he lifts his head, smiles warmly at me. "Christ, you're lovely. You turn me on so much I can't think straight. Now, where were we?"

"You were talking balls, sir." I like to be helpful.

He narrows his eyes at me, and nods slightly. "Ah, yes. Balls." He reaches into his pocket to retrieve the silicone eggs, glances at them rolling innocently across his palm. "So, Miss Byrne, I'd like you to lie back, please, and open your legs wide for me."

Now this is a position I definitely like. I shuffle back onto the bale a little farther, enough to be able to bring my heels up and place them on the edge, and I spread my thighs wide. Nathan maintains eye contact with me as he trails the backs of his fingers along my cleft, from my tight little anus, across my labia and finally circling my clit. He does this slowly, deliberately, several times, a slight smile playing across his lips as he watches me writhe under his hands, feels the moisture gather At last, he slowly inserts just the tip of his finger into my slick, wet channel. I gasp, thrusting upwards for more, but he places his other hand, the one still holding the little balls, across my stomach to keep me in place.

"Keep still, Miss Byrne. I'll tell you when it's time to move." He waits until I'm settled, perfectly still again, before he slides his finger deep inside me. I can't prevent the moan of pleasure that escapes me. My eyes roll shut, but he insists I open them again, refusing to move or touch me again until I do.

"Keep your eyes open, and looking at me, Miss Byrne. I want to watch you unravel. Do you understand?"

"Yes." My voice is just a whisper, but it's enough. He withdraws his finger, only to slide it back again, this time accompanied by two more. I catch my breath again, my eyes widening as he plunges deep.

"Is that good, Eva?"

"Yes." Again I'm whispering.

"You're so hot and wet. And tight. I think you're loving this, aren't you?" He continues to finger-fuck me, curling his longest middle finger to make sure he hits that exact spot on my inner wall to make me convulse and clench around him as the ecstasy builds. "Tell me, Eva, are you loving this as much as I am?"

"Yes. Oh yes." I'm still managing the eye contact, but only with a supreme effort of will, and despite his hand on my stomach, my hips are gyrating wildly. He seems not to mind my movements now, and when he shifts his hand slightly to position his thumb on my clit, rubs firmly, once, twice, that does it. Whatever his instructions I close my eyes as my orgasm bubbles and explodes, and I'm flying. His fingers are still inside me as I clench and squeeze, my inner muscles no longer under my control as the climax takes over. He continues to stroke my clit, drawing every last shudder and tremor from me before at last I'm still again, quiet. He leans forward to kiss my navel before finally sliding his wonderful, clever fingers out of my vagina.

"Well, you're nice and wet now. I don't think we'll need this. At least, not yet." He pulls a tube of lubricant from his other jeans pocket then drops it onto the bale beside me. Talk about coming prepared, quite the Boy Scout. I can't stop the slight smile at the thought, and he catches it.

"Something amusing you, Miss Byrne? Let's see if we can really bring a smile to your face…" And I gasp as he uses the fingers of his left hand to gently part my labia and swiftly slides first one little egg, then its twin, deep into my pussy. He uses his fingers to push them up deep inside me, snugly held within my slick channel. And he's right about the lubricant—my body is utterly unresisting.

He withdraws his fingers, leans over me, still standing between my widespread legs, his hands planted at either side of my shoulders.

"How does that feel?"

I shake my head, unsure. I give a tentative little squeeze, and can feel the balls pressing against my inner walls. It feels…odd, definitely not unpleasant, but not especially remarkable either. "Fine. I think…"

"Fine, you think? Not nearly good enough, Miss Byrne." And with no further ado he lifts me from the bale and plants me back on my feet in front of him. He takes both my hands in his and steps back. I step forward to follow him, and the balls shift.

"Christ!" I splutter, and double up. Nathan laughs, moves to stand behind me and straightens me. The balls lurch sideways again as I move and I gasp. I'd be doubled up again, or on the floor possibly, but for Nathan holding me upright.

"Now how does it feel?" He murmurs the words into my ear, and I lean back against him, let him take my weight as I concentrate on the weird and absolutely wonderful sensations coursing through me. The lovely little eggs tilt and roll, the uneven weights pulling them in one direction then another, every movement of mine causing them to shift again. Instinctively I squeeze and grip them, but even though the eggs themselves might remain still, more or less, the inner weights are still loose and mobile, and causing the most exquisite friction deep inside my vagina.

"Eva, tell me how it feels now." His tone is insistent — my Dom expects an answer.

"Fabulous. Indescribable. It's like… Like…" My words trail away as he steps backwards, drawing me with him, and the eggs give another glorious little tumble inside me. I groan, and suddenly feel an overwhelming urge to stroke my own clit. I start to reach for it, but he anticipates my action and grabs my hand.

"Not yet, my sexy little sub. Maybe later. First there's the matter of your disrespect and disobedience earlier. And you didn't finish what you were saying."

"Please, I need to come. Again. Please let me…"

"No. You'll come when I say so. Now, you walk."

"I can't walk. I can't move a muscle. Every time I do these things move and…"

"I know how they work. I'm wondering about making you walk back to Black Combe with them still inside you. It might take a while, but it'll take your mind off flowers and grass."

"I can't. Please don't..."

"Okay, not all the way home then. But you can manage to stagger over to that water trough over there, and back here. You just need to grip the balls tight. Squeeze them hard and you'll be fine."

I glance up and see the water trough about fifteen feet away. And it might as well be fifteen miles. I don't think I can manage more than one or two steps and stay upright. The sensations are not painful, or uncomfortable. They are simply wonderful. And completely overwhelming.

Gently he pushes me upright until I'm taking my own weight again, then quickly lets go of me, steps around me and over to the target water trough. He stands in front of it, facing me. "Get a grip, girl, and come here."

I recognise that tone, and I know I need to get one foot in front of the other and do this. It's only a few steps, and now at least I know what to expect. Sure enough, the first couple of shuffling paces are difficult, slow-going as I clench convulsively around the wildly rolling and tumbling eggs, instinctively working my inner muscles in an attempt to draw them deeper inside. He's patient, makes no attempt to hurry me as I inch forward, and my confidence quickly grows. Too quickly. The final couple of steps are made at near normal speed, and the Ben Wa balls go into overdrive. I lurch forward, and so does Nathan, catching me before I fall. He sweeps me up and carries me back to the bale of hay where my jacket is still spread out enticingly. He plants me back on my feet, and I lean against the bale, savouring the continuing motion of the balls.

"Right, that's enough exercise for today, I think. Maybe you could wear those around the house in future, get used to the feeling." He catches my look of astonished scorn and chuckles. "Ah, but you'll thank me in later life. It'll do wonders for your pelvic floor."

"Fuck my pelvic floor…" I'm muttering darkly, but he catches it and laughs out loud.

"Not sure that's possible, love. Let me think about it. And that's another piece of disrespect to add to today's tally. Your bottom will be sore. Maybe you should shut up now."

I've opened my mouth to speak again, and what I had in mind to say was far from respectful. He's right, I definitely should shut up now.

I don't, though. "What tally? What did I do?"

"You took the piss when you called me sir. And there was that 'talking balls' comment. And you closed your eyes when I distinctly told you not to. Earlier, when I was finger-fucking you."

"But that was when I came. I couldn't… I mean, how could I—?"

"And I didn't give permission for you to come either, but as I hadn't expressly told you to wait I'm letting that go. Not anymore, though. You'll wait until I tell you it's okay before you climax again. Is that clear? Any questions?"

I shake my head—it all seems fairly clear.

"What are you going to do?" I know he intends to punish me, that at least is obvious. And I'm incredibly aroused now, just thinking about it. I guess I'm really connecting with my submissive side at last. Or maybe it's these bloody balls that are shifting my perspective.

Whatever, I'm distinctly interested in whatever's coming next.

"I'm going to bend you over this nice bale of hay here and spank your bottom. Hard. And you're going to keep perfectly still, because every time you move those balls will shift and roll and you'll be that bit closer to orgasming. And you know you're not allowed to do that, don't you, Eva?"

I gaze at him, my eyes wide. I'm confused, incredibly aroused and somehow managing to be scared as well. I know a spanking is fine, quite nice actually, but with those balls inside me? And not allowed to move? I doubt I'll be able to keep still for long.

He's watching me carefully, sees the myriad of expressions cross my face. "I see you're really starting to get it, this little game of ours. Enjoy, Eva, if you can. Now you can. And if you think you might struggle to obey me about keeping still you can always ask me to tie you up if that would be easier."

I take a moment to think about that then lift my gaze to his. "I... Yes, I think it might be. Please."

He nods then strides across the barn, before returning a few moments later with some rope and a handful of those plastic cable ties you can buy at DIY shops. And I smell a rat. A metaphorical one this time

"How did you know where those were? Did you plan all this?"

He smiles at me, his eyes gleaming wickedly. "Indeed I did, sweetheart. I always do."

"I see. And I suppose you brought a whip or something too."

"No, I'm more of a cane man myself, as you know. Or I used to be. Tom likes whips, though—I could ask him if you like. Hold out your hands, please."

My head still whirling a little from the casual remark about Tom, I dutifully hold my hands out. He deftly loops a cable tie around each wrist, pulls it just tight enough to not allow my hands to slip through, and uses a third to fasten the two plastic loops together. Then he walks around to the other side of the bale and picks up the length of rope. He threads this through the baling cord holding the huge cube of hay together, and looks at me. "Bend over the bale, please, and stretch out your arms."

I do as I'm asked, and he loops the rope between my wrists and around the central connecting cable tie, pulling it tight. I'm neatly fastened in place, my bottom conveniently positioned for spanking, or whatever else he might have in mind. Nathan doesn't move back around, though, not yet. Instead he leans casually on another bale of hay behind him, apparently ready for a chat.

"Safe words, Eva. Are we still using 'red'?"

I nod.

"That's fine, just checking. I was intending to use my hand on that gorgeous little arse of yours, but if you want me to I can probably find something else. Do you have a particular preference?"

I shake my head. "No, whatever you think's best." But my gaze has dropped to his belt, and I can't help wondering...

"Good answer. You are getting into this, aren't you? Why are you staring at my dick? I know I've got a hard-on—but still...?"

"I was just thinking. Wondering if..."

He glances down, sees where my eyes are fixed, on the shiny buckle of his thick leather belt.

"My, we are getting brave. Are you sure about this, sweetheart?"

"Well, not the buckle end, obviously…"

"Obviously."

"And you mustn't hit me too hard."

"Now that's my call, not yours. I work out what you need, and how much of it. You just lie there and accept it. Deal?"

I wait for a moment before answering. Then, my voice remarkably strong, given the circumstances, I give him my response. "Deal."

He starts to unbuckle the belt, slides it slowly back through the loops on his jeans. Once free, he folds the two ends together and waits. I'm sure he still expects me to change my mind, to chicken out. Instead I smile and turn my head to lay my cheek down on the lining of my jacket spread on top of the hay. I'm ready.

I should be scared. Terrified, even. I'm tied down, naked, about to be beaten with a heavy leather belt. Instead, I feel vulnerable. And totally safe. And I realise in one of my light-bulb moments, that this is what trust feels like. And I like it.

My eyes are closed, but I hear his footsteps as he moves around to stand behind me.

"How many can you manage, Eva?"

"It's your punishment. You decide." And I know it'll be all right, whatever he decides on.

"Twenty then. That okay with you?"

"Mmm, twenty seems — fair."

Despite my new-found relaxed attitude, I still squeal when the first stroke lands, harsh and cruel across my left buttock. And I clench, hard, squeezing those lovely little balls inside me. The force of the blow causes me to move, despite being tied in place, shaking and tilting the weighted eggs and causing a delicious ripple to run the entire length of my vagina. Christ, what a sensation. Trust him to know how this would affect me. The 'no orgasm' rule might well be broken, and soon. I'm confused by my responses, but in no doubt at all that I want more.

And I get more. I'm curiously eager for the next stroke, and I'm not disappointed. I squeal again, and again as the third one lands.

"Breathe in between the strokes, and out as each one falls. Let the hay absorb the force. And concentrate on how those balls feel inside you. But remember, you don't come until I tell you to." His tone is low, matter-of-fact. He could be advising me on planting cabbages rather than explaining to me how best to weather a beating and instructing me to resist climaxing. Still, his advice on respiration is useful, and I find it helps. A lot. I manage to control my breathing, and rather than reacting to the sharp pain as each stroke hits me, I find I can let it flow through and past me, into the hay below my body. No amount of breathing control can calm the inner tension caused by those little weighted balls, though, and I'm dangling on the edge of the most explosive climax I think I've ever had. And my experience is now somewhat wider.

It's sort of strange, other-worldly. I can still feel the pain, I'm aware of it, but it no longer matters to me. I begin to feel a little bit as if I were drunk, but the sensation has come on more suddenly than that would. And I'm still thinking straight, I'm sure I am. I feel as though I'm floating, weightless, but still hugging the hay beneath me. I'm aware of the belt landing across my bottom, but it seems to be less frequent now, and I'm sure he's not hitting me so hard. It's enough, but only just.

I realise I've lost count, though I'm sure we must be getting close to twenty. And I'm disappointed. I don't want this to end, this exquisite pain, this heady out of body experience. I recall a line from a song I heard somewhere, and recite it over and over in my head, as if on a loop. *'Hurts so good, hurts so good...'* Now I know what that means.

The beating has stopped, and I feel...cheated. Unfulfilled. I need more, something else, something...

"Open your legs for me, Angel." I feel his strong fingers parting my thighs, and I manage to shuffle my feet out slightly to help. Nathan slides his long fingers between my slick folds, and I think he's about to take away my lovely new toys. I moan in disappointment only to change that to delight as he reaches my clit and stays there, stroking, rubbing, circling the swollen, sensitive nub.

"Come for me, come now, Angel." His voice is low and sexy and sweet, but still he's my Dom and I obey. Gladly. I let it go, and I'm flying again. And I was right—this climax is big, powerful, overwhelming me. My body convulses around the Ben Wa balls, heightening and intensifying the glorious, thrilling tingling that is setting me alight. I cling to the hay under my fingers, shuddering with pleasure as wave after wave of delight engulfs me. I'm moaning, whimpering, absolutely lost in the passion of this moment, which just goes on and on and on.

Eventually, though, it passes, and I'm quiet once more. I'm breathless, my heart still pounding. I lie motionless, waiting for my body to return to normal. At last I regain the power of speech.

"That was wonderful. Thank you."

"It was indeed. And we're not done yet. I think you really need to be fucked right now, wouldn't you agree, Miss Byrne?"

I really can't argue with that. "Yes, that would be nice."

"Wouldn't it just. I intend to fuck you here…" He is circling my anus with his fingers, the tight little rosette quivering under his touch. "Is that all right with you? You have such a nice, tight little arse. I need to sink my cock into it. Now."

"Yes, do it. Please, I need…"

I gasp as he slides one long finger smoothly past the sphincter and into my arse, sinking deep, probing. He withdraws it, only to insert it again, twisting and swirling it inside me. I realise he's working the lubricant inside, as well as easing me open for his penetration. Soon a second finger joins in the fun, then a third. And I'm ready.

I hear the snap of a condom foil breaking, and a few seconds pass as he unrolls the latex over his erection. Then he's behind me nudging my rear entrance with the head of his cock, pressing forward, gentle but firm, slipping inside me. He doesn't thrust at first, just continues to ease his length into me, giving me time to adjust, to accept him. And I'm intensely conscious of the Ben Wa balls rolling and tumbling in my vagina, so close, every movement acutely felt in both places.

At last he's fully inside, his entire length deeply embedded. He leans forward, his lips just behind my ear.

"Are you doing okay, Eva? Is this gentle enough for you?"

"Yes. Yes." My voice is a breathy whisper. "Too gentle. I won't break."

"No, I don't believe you will. Okay then."

He pulls back, almost right the way out, only to plunge forward once more. The balls lurch around inside me, my arse is stretched—I'm impossibly and utterly full. My muscles relax and I'm totally receptive, loving all this, all that he can do for me. I don't believe I've ever felt as good as I do in this moment. I groan, lost in the sensation as he continues to thrust, slowly at first, but gathering pace as his own climax builds.

He reaches around me to find my clit with his skilled fingers, rolling it between his finger and thumb, tugging slightly, squeezing. It's enough, more than enough, and I find myself hurtling into freefall again. This orgasm is less powerful than the previous one, but no less wonderful for that. I revel in it, shuddering with joy as all my senses focus on my core, filled and stimulated beyond my imagining. And moments after the ripples of my own orgasm fade I feel him jerk and stiffen inside me, and hear his muffled "Fuck, Eva, that's bloody wonderful" as the hot surge of his semen fills the condom.

We both lie still, silent, for long minutes. I've no choice about staying put as I'm still tied up, but I wouldn't have moved anyway. Couldn't have, even if the barn caught fire. At last Nathan stirs, pulls carefully out of me, disposes of the condom. I'm puzzled about why he used it, and I try to find the energy to ask. And fail, distracted no doubt by the sweet sensation of the Ben Wa balls being eased from my body.

I make no attempt to prise open my eyelids as I listen to the rustle of Nathan rearranging his clothing, hardly disturbed in the first place, as usual, apart from his belt, of course. He moves back around to the front and uses a small pocket knife to slice through the plastic cable ties around my wrists, and rubs my stiff hands briskly. The cable ties weren't tight, but I've been clenching the hay tightly, digging my fingers into the bale. Satisfied that I've regained at least some movement he rolls me onto my back to kiss me, at first just feathering his lips over mine, then deepening. I manage to lift my arm enough to drape it across the back of his neck, but that's the sum of my available energy for now.

His kiss is sensual, but not demanding. It's more of a 'thank you' than a 'give me, now', and I'm once more flooded with a blend of lust and love, not sure which is in the ascendancy. It really doesn't matter in any case. He's mine, I'm his. End of.

It seems much later, but in reality is only a few minutes, I suppose, and Nathan's passing me my clothes.

"Shall we go and find Tom? He's had enough time to make the coffee by now." Nathan's voice is lightly teasing as he watches me struggle to fasten my bra, eventually reaching behind me to do the honours. On the rare occasions I bother to wear one, I usually do that fasten in front and pull it around thing, but not when he's watching. It doesn't seem elegant somehow.

"He might not be back yet," I answer as I'm shoving my legs back into my jeans.

"He came back about twenty minutes ago. You were obviously otherwise occupied in subspace and didn't hear the Land Rover."

I glance up at him, surprised. "What? I was what?"

"Subspace. In the zone. You looked to be enjoying yourself so I let it drag on for a while. Extended to thirty strokes, although not so heavy towards the end."

I'd thought so. I hadn't been dreaming then. He did slow down, turned the dial back a bit. But the memory is distinctly hazy. He passes me my T-shirt and I tug it over my head.

"What do you mean, 'in the zone'? What's that?"

"Also known as subspace. You can Google it later."

Too right I will!

"It's a sort of trance triggered by a rush of pheromones. It happens to some submissives when they really manage to connect with whatever's happening to them. I'm told it's very nice. Was it?"

I try to recall, but the memory keeps dancing away. "I—yes, I think so. I can't really remember. It was a bit like being drunk."

"But cheaper. And no hangover afterwards. Probably kinder to your liver too, though your bum might not agree."

I pat at my bottom, surprised at how comfortable it actually feels. "I'm hardly sore at all. Did you say thirty strokes?"

"Yes. I know we agreed twenty, but I took an executive decision because you were having a good time. Is that okay? In future, if you don't want me to extend a scene, I won't. When you're in subspace you're in no position to argue or make decisions, so it's good if I know beforehand what you want me to do."

I have no hesitation in my answer. "Do what you think best. I trust you. Absolutely."

He smiles and winks at me, and in that moment I know I've got it. Not just the trust thing, though that's a monumental breakthrough for me, but also this sense of comfort, of being fine with myself. For perhaps the first time ever I'm actually comfortable inside my own skin. I feel beautiful, I feel cared for, valued. Respected.

I suppose he's only telling me what my mother has for years, and what my father did when I was little. But parents are biased, and it's in their job description to say nice things. Now I find myself thinking that my parents may well have been biased, but that doesn't make them wrong. I *am* okay.

My self-esteem soaring, I'm happy to take Nathan's hand as we stroll back across the cobbles towards the farmhouse, ignoring the frantic, furious cackling of the geese, livid at our reappearance.

"Where's Barney?" I ask, noticing that our huge furry chaperone has deserted us.

"Probably inside, with Tom." Nathan is shrugging back into his jacket, retrieved from the door handle as we came out into the bright sunlight.

"Oh God, he'll know we're here then. But, why didn't he come looking for us? He might have just walked into the barn. Shit!" I don't suppose he'd have been mentally scarred for life, but still, I would have been mortified if he'd seen what we were up to among his hay bales.

"He knew where we were. And what we were doing. He'll have spotted my jacket on the door handle so he stayed out of the way—tact is Tom's middle name. And he wouldn't like it much if I disturbed him in the middle of a scene. We have an understanding, you might say." Nathan's casual confidence in the face of my near panic at the prospect of discovery is suspicious—he knows something I don't. And I recall the comment earlier, about Tom's whips.

"Does he really have whips? Tom, I mean."

"Oh, yes. A fine collection. You've seen them, at my apartment. I'm not sure if he has any here—maybe a riding crop or two…"

I'm astonished. "Your apartment! Why would Tom's stuff be there?"

"He uses it sometimes. A lot of the equipment is his." He smiles at my incredulous expression.

"But... Tom seems so nice."

"Ah, sweetheart, don't we all? Don't we all?"

My head is still reeling as we walk into the house—Nathan doesn't even bother to knock—to be greeted by Barney and two bouncing border collies, and one very nice Mr Tom Shore, who's already poured us both a coffee.

* * * *

It's now Sunday evening, four whole days—and nights—later and there have been no further opportunities to be alone with Nathan. Consequently I am very, very desperate, and to make matters worse Nathan has an eight o'clock meeting in the morning in Leeds so he's leaving at six. He won't be back all week, not until Friday evening. I've no idea how I'm going to last. So here I am, lying on my own bed, staring at the darkness and seriously considering a DIY job. Nathan showed me how in one of our more memorable erotic encounters, encouraging me to touch myself while he watched. A useful skill and one I'm going to have to put to use.

The click of the door stills my hand before I've done much more than shove my pyjama shorts off and run my fingers across my still perfectly smooth and hairless body, reaching for the sweet little button nestling in there. I glance across to see a narrow slit of light, widening as I watch. Nathan slips through the door, closing it softly behind him.

"If I fuck you very, very gently will you promise me you won't scream?"

"I'll promise you anything at all. Just do it, please."

"I like a woman who plays hard to get." And in another moment he's demonstrating just how hard he can get as well. I manage not to scream, but it's touch and go as he takes off his jeans and slips into bed beside me, taking only moments to check my readiness before he slides into my very wet, very hot and very willing body. His mouth on mine swallows my whimpers and moans of pure joy as the pleasure builds, mounts and quickly spirals away leaving me helpless to do anything other than go with it. My first orgasm is there in a matter of seconds, then he slows, delicately withdrawing and thrusting as I gasp under him, boneless, welcoming, and very, very grateful.

He is unhurried and I manage two more climaxes before he finally shudders, swears violently, and I feel the hot wash of his semen filling me. God I love that sensation. He rolls onto his back, holding me tight and carrying me with him so I find myself on top. I frame his beautiful face in my hands and kiss him.

"How long can you stay?"

"I'm getting up at around half five, but until then I'm all yours. What plans do you have for me?"

"I plan to spend all night making love with you." One raised eyebrow indicates he has noted my choice of word, but he doesn't take issue. Progress. "But what about Rosie?"

"Rosie's fast asleep. And even if I have to break our agreement and gag you to keep you quiet I needed you. I couldn't go another day without this, without you. I don't appreciate sneaking around in my own home, but… I was a desperate man."

"Tell me about it. Later." Pushing myself up to straddle him I deliberately squeeze my inner muscles to get his full attention centred where I want it. He groans and I am rewarded with the sensation of something solid, hardening, filling me. In moments his cock is rigid again and settled deep within me, as I sink down onto him, taking all of him. I gyrate my hips slowly, experimenting with the sensation of fullness, of being stretched tight around him as his size swells. I have a moment of panic as he seems so much bigger this time, but his hands on my hips hold me in place as I adjust.

"Take it slow, sweetheart. A little at a time. You set the rhythm." He's never been wrong yet so I gather my confidence, in him and in me, and I relax around him. He steadies me as I start to move, using my knees and upper thighs to push my body upwards and let his cock slide out of me, almost the whole way, then back down to take him fully inside again. It feels wonderful, the friction hot and moist as our bodies glide against each other, every nerve ending on red alert. My clitoris is so swollen it is rubbing against Nathan with every stroke, but it's not enough so I start to stroke myself there. Nathan realises what I am up to, what I need, and obligingly spreads his palms wide, opening his hands to place both thumbs over my swollen, throbbing clit so I can rub myself hard against them with each stroke. Fabulous. Absolutely bloody fantastic.

Aroused almost beyond bearing I squeeze tighter, just because I can and for the joy of seeing Nathan's beautiful features scrunch in ecstasy and know it's me doing it, me in control. I realise this is the first time I've been on top, the dominant partner. Nathan seems perfectly happy with our role reversal if his groans of pure lust are any indication, his fingers now digging into my bottom to encourage me to pick up the pace.

I do, pumping hard to wring every last sliver of pleasure for myself out of his cock, and his perfectly positioned thumbs. I work myself on him, grinding my hips against him greedily. Nathan lets me, making no attempt to take over or increase the pace. This is my show. My own climax is almost here, hovering just a fraction away and I thrust, rub and squeeze him hard, grabbing at orgasm, until I tumble over the edge. Only then, as my body goes slack above him does Nathan take the reins. He thrusts sharply upwards, now rolling his thumbs over my swollen clit to make sure my own orgasm is drawn out for as long as possible, before with a few more sharp thrusts he comes himself. I fall forward, collapsing across his chest and he holds me, stroking my back, my hair, my bottom as our heartbeats return to normal.

I have never been more content in my life. I fall asleep, still on top of him.

Chapter Ten

"I'm going, babe. Kiss me."

The soft voice wakes me and I open my eyes dreamily to find myself looking into Nathan's deep brown gaze. He is crouching beside me, his face close to mine. His lips curl softly and I return the smile as he strokes my hair. He must have been up a while as he's showered and fully dressed, his usual smart and businesslike persona in dark grey trousers, neatly pressed, a crisp white shirt and pink and grey striped tie. His expensive black leather shoes are gleaming as usual. His long hair is slicked back into his customary business ponytail. Just fucked he does not look. And I know I do.

I push myself up on one elbow, realising as his eyes drop to caress my breasts that I am still naked. Well, why not, after all? I make no attempt to cover up as, obedient, I reach for him. I kiss him, as instructed and using all my new-found skills I inject as much passion and longing as I can. Which is not insubstantial these days. I slip my tongue between his lips, tasting, testing, exploring, combing my fingers through his hair and deliberately messing up his neat and still slightly damp ponytail. He doesn't seem to object and returns my kiss with a little tongue-tangling of his own. His hands are on my breasts and I find myself on my back, the duvet pushed to my waist as he breaks the kiss to take my nipple and most of my breast in his mouth. I lie back, delighted, and gasp as he grazes his teeth across the sensitive peak.

Reluctantly, and to my intense disappointment, he lifts his head. "Shit, I wish I could stay. You are the most gorgeous thing to wake up to."

"Right back at you," I respond. "Can't you be late? Just a bit late? This wouldn't take long…"

"It would to do properly. And no, I can't be late, you insatiable little hussy. I have a roomful of developers and their lawyers due in my office at eight. I have to be there. But I would definitely prefer to be here fucking you as you so richly deserve and obviously want."

Giving in to the inevitable, I smile and sit up to see him off properly. Kneeling on the edge of the bed I put my arms around his neck and hug him tight. "Hurry back. I'll miss you." The words are whispered in his ear as he tightens his arms around my naked back. "I love the way you wake me, and I wish you could do that every day. "

"Now there's a thought to work with. And I'll miss you too, Angel. Kiss Rosie for me, too."

"I will, but I'm not sure where kissing my pupils is to be found in the violin tutor's handbook."

"I doubt if fucking their daddies is in there either, but your unorthodox approach is one I find most refreshing, Miss Byrne. Now, I'm going. I'll see you tomorrow evening. Keep everything warm for me."

With one last quick kiss and a soft pat on my bum he

is standing, walking away. He winks at me as he gently closes the door behind him.

Unable to resist I leap out of bed and stand by the window as he leaves the house. I see his car, the sleek, purring Audi, glide away across the gravel of the driveway. I wait by the window watching the small portion of the lane I can see from my room, and after a couple of minutes I see the car sweep past and I know he's gone.

I've been alone, isolated, all my life but I'm feeling consciously lonely for the first time ever. The house feels empty without him in it and I rapidly calculate how many minutes it will be before I see him again. Two thousand two hundred and twenty, at least. If he's not held up. Pathetic.

I know I won't be able to settle back to sleep so I head for the shower. Alone.

* * * *

Despite missing Nathan like crazy I've had an absolutely brilliant time with Rosie for the last couple of days, just the two of us much of the time as Mrs Richardson has been busy on a mass baking project for the Oakworth village fair. Apparently she has ambitions regarding the best fruitcake contest, and this is serious stuff indeed. Rosie and I have been left to our own devices, only called upon to test and evaluate the various approaches to the art of cakery. We are stern critics, and between us we do appear to know a thing or two about what makes a decent cake. Our input seems to be appreciated and after much trial and error, tasting and finger-licking, Mrs Richardson's strategy is in place, the recipe refined, the ingredients lined up ready for the big day.

Apart from our usual morning efforts with the violin—I do intend to at least attempt to deliver what I'm paid for—we've walked miles and miles over the moors, Barney bounding alongside us with his tongue lolling out. He seems able to spot a rabbit at two hundred metres and is forever taking off after them. He's just too big and daft and noisy to ever manage to catch anything, but he loves the chase. Rosie took me to Top Withens, the now ruined farmhouse that is supposed to have been the inspiration for Emily Brontë's *Wuthering Heights*. Standing there on the windswept hillside I could well believe it. I half expected Heathcliff to pop out from behind a dry-stone wall at any moment. And my imaginary Heathcliff bears an uncanny resemblance to Nathan Darke, though I'm not telling Rosie that.

We went bowling yesterday evening, then sloped off to McDonalds for a quick gut-rotting quarter-pounder. No doubt Nathan will have something to say, but we both needed the comfort food. Today it's raining again so we're tucked up indoors with our violins and a chess set, alternating between the two. For a little girl, Rosie is very good company for a geeky oddball like me. And Nathan is due back in three and a bit hours— only a hundred and eighty-nine minutes to go.

I hear my phone trilling away under a cushion on Nathan's big squashy sofa in the lounge, which we have commandeered as our practice studio. After some digging around I manage to extricate it and press the reply button, expecting to hear my mother's voice. She's become most insistent of late that I explain properly and fully just what I'm doing here in Yorkshire, exactly where and exactly with whom. I'm taking her calls, but no way am I telling her about Nathan.

But it's not her. It's Nathan. And the news is bad, bad, *bad*.

"Sweetheart, I've got to go to Ankara. Tonight. I'm on a flight from Manchester at eight forty this evening and I'm on my way to the airport now."

"What? Why?"

"Remember your dear friend Ahmet?"

I have to think for a moment. "Ahmet, right…"

"He fell from some scaffolding. About four storeys, apparently. He's in a bad way and the authorities there suspect it wasn't an accident. Apparently he made himself very unpopular insisting on high spec materials and such like—remember the row you got involved in that day you came into my office? Anyway the word is one of the disgruntled suppliers arranged for him to take a little fall."

"Bloody hell. Poor Ahmet. Will he be okay?"

"Not sure. But the least I can do is get out there and visit him, and his family. And take charge at the site until we can get another foreman who's not corrupt or incompetent. I'm hoping to be back by the middle of next week. Will you be okay?"

"Me? Yes, of course I will. I'll miss you and so will Rosie. But we're okay. Just you take care of yourself, though. What if they have a go at you?"

"I don't scramble up scaffolding as a rule, love. But I know what you mean and I'll be on the lookout. I'll phone you when I get there. Let you know how Ahmet is."

"Tell him I'm rooting for him. He sounded so nice."

"I'll tell him. Will you explain to Rosie and Grace?"

"Yes. Nathan…"

"What is it?"

"I… I'll miss you. Please hurry back."

"I'll miss you too, Eva."

There are a few moments of awkward silence as we both seem to be fumbling around for the words we need. Eventually Nathan breaks the deadlock.

"Bye, love. See you soon." And with a click he is gone.

* * * *

It's been five days and Nathan is still stuck in downtown Ankara. He's been on the phone every evening and it seems Ahmet is likely to be okay, eventually, sort of. He has a broken collarbone, several broken ribs and a smashed wrist. It'll be a while before he's fit for a building site again, if ever, and Nathan thinks he might not be able to work in construction anymore. I gather it's not all bad, though — apparently Ahmet's brother-in-law grows tomatoes in a poly-tunnel somewhere down on the Mediterranean coast and he's been nagging Ahmet to consider a career change. Strange how life turns out sometimes.

Nathan is supervising the construction for the time being, and has ordered a full inspection of all work completed to date to make sure it complies with his specifications. It's a slow job it seems and there is no immediate prospect of him being able to get home.

Rosie and me both miss him, but we're having a decent time together. We went along to the Oakworth Fair to cheer Mrs Richardson on in the Great Cake Challenge. She came second, an improvement of seven places from her position last year. She seemed delighted.

And I won the 'Guess How Many Smarties In The Jar' prize. I suppose there are some who'd say I cheated, or at least didn't properly enter into the spirit of the game. I invested a quid in a tube of Smarties at the sweet stall, worked out how much volume twenty of them took up and the rest was simple mental arithmetic. I got the answer right to within two Smarties. Not much point being a mathematical wizard if you can't use your talent to win a year's supply of Smarties, in my book. And Rosie was over the moon.

We've done our fair share of moors walking, and even went out for a moonlit hike on Sunday evening. We lay on our backs in the bracken, staring up at the night sky, and I pointed out some more of its wonders to Rosie. We spotted one particularly bright star, which we agreed must be her mummy. Rosie told me she remembers her mummy a little bit, but only ever as being ill. She doesn't remember much at all before she went to live with Nathan. She was sad when her mummy died, but not frightened because she had a daddy by then. She told me the best thing ever to happen in her whole life was the day she was a bridesmaid when her daddy married her mummy. The next best thing was the day they went to the dog's home and found Barney. And the next best thing was me coming to teach her violin. God, what an accolade! I could hardly speak for the lump in my throat.

We've been swimming — well, me splashing around in the shallow end with Rosie really — but we had fun. And all three of us went to the cinema and then to Nando's for supper. And today Rosie and I nipped down into Keighley in Mrs Richardson's car to buy a birthday card and present for a friend's party Rosie is going to next weekend. She's so excited, chattering away about the party, the horse riding Barbie we've bought as a present, her new teacher at school, violin concerts we could perform for her daddy, the chicks she's hoping might emerge soon from under Tracey or

Beaker, her pet chickens. My thoughts have, I admit, wandered to my own more private version of performing for her daddy, and I'm listening somewhat selectively to the constant stream of little girl consciousness as we let ourselves in through the back door expecting to be greeted by the sweet aroma of Mrs Richardson's lamb hotpot.

Alas, no. We look at each other in unspoken puzzlement. No simmering dish of juicy hotpot awaits us on the Aga. Indeed, there's no sign of Mrs Richardson, or our lunch at all. What there is, however, is a very agitated Barney, pacing around the room and whining.

Ignoring the dog, Rosie is more worried about her stomach. "She's gone out..." she announces matter-of-factly. "What'll we have for our dinner? I'm so hungry..."

Somewhat puzzled by Barney's antics but still pretty famished myself I'm already peering optimistically into the fridge — well, you never know, there might be a hotpot in there waiting for us to warm it up. Perhaps we misunderstood what Mrs Richardson said as we were leaving this morning. It occurs to me that she can't have gone very far — we borrowed her car. Rosie heads off up to her room to compare horsey Barbie to her own not inconsiderable collection of anorexic but remarkably busty plastic lovelies before wrapping it up. As soon as she opens the door to the hallway Barney is through and shooting upstairs, his huge paws pounding along the landing overhead. I feel the first stirring of alarm as I'm debating between attempting to conjure up cheese toasties or cracking open a tin of tomato soup — my culinary skills are not impressive, I think we've all recognised that, when I hear a gut-wrenching shriek from upstairs. Rosie's voice, shrill with panic and terror, bouncing off the walls.

"Eva! *Eva!* Come quick. Nana's dead!"

About the Author

Until 2010, Ashe was a director of a regeneration company before deciding there had to be more to life and leaving to pursue a lifetime goal of self-employment.

Ashe has been an avid reader of women's fiction for many years—erotic, historical, contemporary, fantasy, romance—you name it, as long as it's written by women, for women. Now, at last in control of her own time and working from her home in rural West Yorkshire, she has been able to realise her dream of writing erotic romance herself.

She draws on settings and anecdotes from her previous and current experience to lend colour, detail and realism to her plots and characters, but her stories of love, challenge, resilience and compassion are the conjurings of her own imagination. She loves to craft strong, enigmatic men and bright, sassy women to give them a hard time—in every sense of the word.

When she's not writing, Ashe's time is divided between her role as resident taxi driver for her teenage daughter, and caring for a menagerie of dogs, cats, rabbits, tortoises and a hamster.

Ashe Barker loves to hear from readers. You can find her contact information, website details and author profile page at http://www.totallybound.com.

Totally Bound Publishing

Home of Erotic Romance